CASUALTIES

CASUALTIES

Joyce Becker Lee

Tortoise Books
Chicago

FIRST EDITION, MARCH, 2023

Published in the United States by Tortoise Books

www.tortoisebooks.com

ASIN: B0BHBWQ13C
ISBN-13: 978-1-948954-75-4

For my children, who encourage,
and my grandchildren, who inspire

Contents

Casualties

Pain can be lessened when expected, and Dinah Goldman had come to expect pain, so the sting was palliated when only a few of her peers accepted her party invitations. Still, rejection is never easy to take, especially for a teenage girl who can't quite comprehend bigotry, nor why she should be an object of exclusion.

Her parents had suggested the party, and Dinah had gone along, dutifully helping her mother plan, as though nothing had changed. As though her junior year hadn't been one of burgeoning alienation dotted with snide "Jew" comments, both overheard and overt. Dinah viewed with alarm the change from the Depression's "pull together" attitude to the wartime anti-Semitism that seemed to permeate tiny Plum Grove, maybe all of Wisconsin, even the entire country.

The remarks had come with greater frequency and bitterness as the war had gone on, as each new gold star appeared in some grieving family's window. Sometimes the antipathy was blatant, as when Floyd refused to serve her at the ice cream parlor or when Mrs. Ryan had referred to "you people" at their weekly knitting circle, the place where women gathered to knit socks and, later, stump covers for the soldiers. But more often, those around her said covert comments just loud enough for her to hear in the school halls, the lunchroom, and behind her back in classes.

Her older siblings had escaped the persecution: Becky was married and living in Chicago, and Harry was an army doctor in a Washington military hospital. Dinah had suggested that she live with Becky and go to school in the city, but her father had been skeptical.

"Why would you leave? This land represents everything your grandfather came here for. Plum Grove is our home."

"*Kotchkala,* our people have been bullied and pushed out for centuries." Her mother's eyes were sad, far away, her face set in steel. "No, we have every right to be here, and we're not running away."

They don't see it, Dinah thought. Her father owned the bank, and people were friendly to him because of that. She found herself only invited to parties because of her father's position. But since the Shore Club opened on Plum Lake, bluntly stating, "no Negroes, no Jews," even those invitations had dwindled.

"I'm sorry, Dinah, but my parents want my party to be at the Shore Club" became a familiar, convenient excuse. Dinah's home on what had once been the family farm sat on the same lake as the new club. Dinah spent many evenings sitting on a rock at the family's little beach, staring at the distant lights and listening to the music that came wafting over the water, taunting her, holding acceptance just beyond her reach.

And now, her parents wanted her to have a party for those who excluded her.

"Invite your whole class," her mother suggested.

"They won't come," Dinah protested.

Her father's eyes turned to cold steel as he patted his daughter's cheek.

"Some will come," he said.

Her optimism rising at his words, she invited all thirty-seven junior class members; only a few accepted, but even that small number heartened her. She felt, knew, that this was the beginning, that this tiny bit of acceptance would lead to more.

Now that small group was clustered in her back yard beneath the soft glow of paper lanterns her father had strung through the trees, and Dinah thought maybe he had been right, that she did belong there after all. He seemed so at ease, flipping hamburgers and joking with the kids. She could see the chain of the silver mezuzah she knew he always wore tucked inside through his sport shirt's open collar. Guilt shot through her—her silver star, a gift from her grandmother on her *bat mitzvah*, lay hidden in the little box on her dresser.

Dinah's best friend Alice was there, of course, and Alice's boyfriend, Fred, also a plank in Dinah's small security raft. June and Betty were there, too, as well as June's boyfriend Jimmy. Dinah had figured they'd come, as they had been friends since childhood, and they were always nice to her. But she was a little surprised to see Jerry and Carl. Popular football players and class leaders, they had never been that friendly, but their appearance was as good as a suit of armor, proof that the crack in the wall of ostracism was widening. And of course, George, the most important one, would be coming later, after work. She'd spent a significant amount of time across from him in chemistry class trying out different smiles, different ways of batting her eyelashes. He'd said he'd come, promising, "I'll be late, but I'll be there."

Here, then, was her turning point. They'd all see that she wasn't any different from them, that there was no reason to shun her, and they'd convince the others. All she needed was that first boost, and then things would go back to the way they had been before the war, before the hate, before Jews became the "reason" American boys were being killed in Europe.

Everyone seemed to be having a good time. Alice helped Dinah play hostess, flitting from the house to the yard, carrying food bowls, trading teasing jokes with Dinah's father, just like always. Dinah cringed when Jimmy said, "So these dogs are *kosher*? Gosh, they taste just like real food!" But Mr. Goldman laughed at the remark, and Dinah decided Jimmy wasn't nasty, just ignorant, and she began to relax. Who cared about the others who snubbed her? These people were her true friends. She couldn't wait for George to get there. Dinah vowed to get him alone in the moonlight, her blood flowing warm at thoughts almost too delicious to bear.

After supper, her parents drifted discreetly into the house, leaving the teens to dance and listen to records in the early summer twilight. Jerry peeked through the screen to check on the adults' proximity, then reached in and carefully closed the back door.

"Okay, we can start the fun," Jerry said. He ran to Jimmy's car and returned with a large bottle, which he went around pouring into everyone's glasses.

Dinah glanced at the house. She could hear the faint merriment from the radio in the den and her parents' slightly louder laughter in response through the closed door. Well, it wouldn't hurt, she thought. They'd never know. She tried the amber liquid Jerry poured in her glass and made a face at the bitter taste. She was used to the sweet wine her family drank on Friday nights, and the sharpness made her breath blow hot through her throat and nose. The other girls sipped daintily while the boys, especially Jerry and Carl, pounded down drink after drink.

"Now, this is a party!" Jerry laughed, tossing back the last of the bottle's contents.

Carl gazed off into the deepening darkness at the water beyond. "Hey, Dinah, does your yard go all the way to the lake?"

"Yes," Alice answered for her. "They've got a beach, too."

Carl grabbed Dinah's hand and pulled her to her feet. "Show us."

"We're waiting for George," she protested.

"Ah, he'll find us."

"Sure," Dinah said. "Come on."

The back lawn sloped gently to the lake. "Wow, you've got a lot of land," Betty said.

"This was our cow pasture," Dinah said. "My grandpa was a farmer."

"So, how come your dad's not a farmer?" Jimmy asked.

"I guess he just wanted something else."

"You mean something better?" Carl's voice sounded strained.

"My dad's a farmer," Jimmy said, his tone slightly slurred. "An' I'll be one, too."

"I didn't mean—" Dinah began.

"We know what you meant," Carl said, and Dinah tried to ignore the muted resentment in his voice.

They followed the path to the small patch of beach. Fat clouds lazily obscured the moon, their ragged edges tipped in moonlight silver; the shoreline on either side of the pale sand disappeared in the shadows of trees and untrimmed brush. A soft light spread above the horizon, and music drifted on the cool night air from the club across the lake.

"There must be a party at the club tonight," Dinah said.

"Purdy's having his graduation party there," Betty said. "I'm his girl. I should've been there."

"Well, why weren't you?" Dinah asked, unsure if she was more surprised at Betty's presence than Purdy's obvious perfidy.

"My folks said I had to come here,"

"*Had* to? Why would they say that?" Dinah couldn't imagine her parents forcing her to go anywhere she didn't want to go.

Betty didn't say anything, but Jimmy answered for her, his voice low. "Your dad told our parents that if we didn't come tonight, he might call in their loans."

"What?" Dinah felt her lungs suddenly squeeze tight.

"Yeah," Carl said. "I'da been there now, too, if your dad hadn't threatened to repossess our car."

"I'm sorry, Dinah," Fred said. "I came because of Alice, but that's pretty much everyone else's story." He grabbed Alice and kissed her.

"Shhh," Alice giggled, and they started moving off toward the brush-choked path.

Dinah felt a *click* in her brain. "No, my father wouldn't have done that."

"Oh, no? Then how do you figure we'd come to a Jew party instead of Purdy's?" Jerry's laugh was high and mean.

"Shut up," June muttered, smacking his arm. "Di, don't listen to him. He's just a jerk."

"I'll show you a jerk. C'mere, Baby," Jimmy pulled June into the darkness at the edge of the clearing.

Dinah's thoughts rushed. Her father wouldn't have done that—would he? Didn't he understand—No, she had to make it right. She turned to Betty.

"Go. You should be with Purdy tonight." Betty hesitated, then touched Dinah's arm gently and disappeared up the path. Dinah suddenly felt very tired.

"You can all go if you want."

"Hmmm. Might be difficult," Carl said. When Dinah looked back, she saw she was alone with Carl and Jerry.

"Where—?" she started, looking around.

"Oh, Fred and Alice went that way," Carl indicated the brush to their right, "and Jimmy and June are—wherever." Since we rode with them, I guess we're stuck here for a while. With you."

They were standing very close to her, and Dinah moved away. "Well, just wait until the moon comes out again," she said, hoping her voice didn't give away any discomfort. "My beach is so beautiful in the moonlight. We could go wading or—or something."

"*My* beach, huh? So, you own a while fucking beach!" Carl's voice in the darkness had a strange, brittle edge.

Jerry's voice growled. "Show-off Jew."

The word was a fetid belch in the darkness, and Dinah felt the darkness pressing on her eyes, her mouth, her throat, palpable enough to make her wave her hand across her face as though to brush away a spider web. She felt a sudden, overwhelming sadness.

"You got a better house, a better yard, even your own damn beach, huh? No mortgage hanging over your head!" Carl muttered.

"Hey, what else you think she's got that's better?" The two voices were interchangeable now, the figures shadows in the darkness. One moved in closer behind Dinah, and she felt fingers tickle the nape of her neck, fear choking her breath, constricting her words.

"Let's go back." She wrenched away from the clutching paw. "Alice, June!" she called, turning toward the path, but a solid form blocked the way. She turned away, but her arm was grabbed and jerked backward, and a sharp pain shot through her wrested shoulder.

"Not so fast, Baby." The darkness emboldened the faceless voice. Was it Carl or Jerry? She couldn't tell. Dinah felt their anger thrust against her, rooting her feet to the ground even though her brain screamed to run.

Another hand grabbed her other arm and yanked her around the other way; she winced in pain.

"Leave me alone," she demanded, determined to find her control. She backed away from the encroaching figures but was stopped by one of the boys behind her snaking his arms around her waist. She slapped the prodding hands and pushed out, her kitten-heeled sandals sinking into the sand. She slipped them off, instinctively preparing for flight.

"You think you're so hot. You and your big-shot parents."

"What? No, listen—" Dinah felt dizzy. This wasn't real and couldn't be happening. She was shoved forward, more roughly now, caught by strong arms.

Forcing herself to look up at the owner of the imprisoning arms, Dinah saw it was Jerry. His face triggered a flash remembrance of a conversation overheard, and she cried in desperation, "Jerry Riemer! My dad was kind to your folks! He let them miss house payments."

Jerry jerked away at that, seeming surprised. She felt a swell of strength from this sudden upper hand, and her voice came out a sneer. "No one else would help them," she said to the darkness. "You owe keeping your house to Jews!"

The moment she said the words, she knew she'd made a mistake.

Jerry's head snapped up, and she saw his snarl, his teeth flashing through the dark.

"Liar!" His voice was strangled. "Jew lies!" He grabbed Dinah again and tossed her to Carl, who shoved her backward, so she fell into the brush. She struggled to get up, hearing her dress tear from thorny branches that scratched her bare arms and legs.

Jerry laughed. "Hey, y'know, she's kinda cute. For a Jew."

Strong hands pushed her down on the sand, pinning her as Jerry's sudden weight pressed down the length of her body, his face pushing against her own, his breath filling her nose.

She struggled, gasping, but the weight was too great. She felt rough hands pulling up her skirt, tugging at her panties.

Horror had swallowed her scream. She struggled to push away, but firm hands pinned her shoulders to the ground.

"Stop, please!" Dinah managed to croak, kicking wildly against the hands that were pulling her thighs apart. "Please!" Rough hands tore away her lace underpants, fingers rubbed her inner leg, then probed higher, ragged fingernails scratching the soft tissue. She felt a searing pain, and she screamed, her shriek like that of an animal, bouncing back at her through the darkness.

A hand clamped down on her mouth.

"Shut up and enjoy it," Jerry growled.

He began moving, rubbing against her struggles, his voice grunting in her ear. She heard Carl's laughter as though through a tunnel. Looking up, she saw the moon break from behind a cloud, flooding the shore with soft, pearly light. Beyond, the lake sparkled with a million dots dancing on its rippled surface in time to a rhumba beat from across the water. She twisted her face away and screamed again.

"Get off her!" a voice shouted. Dinah felt the hand drop away. Twisting her head, she saw George come bounding down the path, yelling and swinging his arms. She felt Jerry's weight abruptly lift, heard George's voice yelling, saw him shove Jerry, who stumbled and sat on the ground laughing.

"What the hell's the matter with you?" George growled.

Jerry laughed weakly. "Take it easy, Hero. I didn't spoil her for you."

Following the screams and shouts, the absent couples appeared, and Dinah heard Jerry mutter something about "just having a little fun."

"Jeez! Di!" Alice muttered, and Dinah felt hands pulling her skirt down from where it was crumpled around her waist, wrapping fabric around her clenched fist. Dinah stared, dazed, at the scrap of her panties, a failed guardian.

"C'mon," Alice whispered. "You're okay, they didn't—" She turned and hissed at the boys, "Get out of here!"

"Party's over," Carl said, his voice shaking slightly. "Let's go."

"We can still make it to Purdy's." It was Fred. "Who's riding with me?"

As the group moved away, Jerry ran back to where Dinah and Alice stood staring after them. "You don't tell anyone about this," he hissed. "No one would believe you, anyhow. And if they did, they wouldn't care." From a distance, Fred called, "You coming, Alice?"

Alice had collected Dinah's sandals and now thrust them into her hands.

"They were just goofing around, you know," Alice whispered. "No harm done." She looked after the retreating crowd. "I'd better go."

Dinah stared at her, unbelieving. "You're leaving?"

"Fred's waiting. You're okay. I'll call you tomorrow and tell you about Purdy's party," Alice said, then called out, "Hey, Freddy, wait for me!" She gave Dinah a quick peck on the cheek. "It was a fun party, Di. 'Bye."

As she watched Alice's retreating back, Dinah detected a figure off to the side. It was George, still there, and he moved toward her. His beautiful face in the moonlight was full of concern and something else—a promise that was now spoiled. Pity succeeded where hatred had failed, and Dinah began to cry.

"Go," she sobbed.

"No, I—Let me help you."

"Just go." Her voice fell to a hoarse whisper. "Please."

He hesitated a moment. "I'll wait for you at the top of the path," he said, then turned and disappeared up the path. Dinah stood in the sand, waiting for the feeling to return to her hands and feet. Warm wetness trickled between her legs; she pulled up her skirt and, wincing, wiped herself with the torn underpants. When Dinah withdrew the white cloth, she saw it dotted with dark splotches that gleamed wetly in the silvery light. The roar of the cars by the house faded, and she stood between the water and the moonlight, the gentle splat of waves against her ankles in counterpoint to the lively music from the other side of the lake. She turned away from the path and took a different way home.

The radio was still playing inside the house when she stepped up to the porch, folding her skirt to hide the tear. In the den, her parents turned with expectant faces as she entered, her mother's eyes scanning Dinah's face.

"They're all gone," Dinah said.

"They seemed to have had a good time," her mother said.

"They did," her father replied and turned to smile at her. He had taken off his shirt, and the silver mezuzah hung free over his undershirt. "It was a nice party, wasn't it?"

She lowered her eyes. "Yes. Thank you."

"That's what parents are for."

Dinah looked up. He was smiling—smugly? She wasn't sure. What did he think? That he could force them to be her friends? She wanted to cry, to scream, to blame him, but there was something else in the depths of his eyes: self-deception and secrets and even fear beneath an epidermis of confidence. He was no giant, just a man like any other, a little stooped of the shoulder, trying to live in his world, treading water to keep from drowning.

But she didn't want to swim anymore.

From the stairs, Dinah looked down at them, suddenly seeming small and far away as though standing in a deep hole. "I want to go live with Becky in the fall and finish school in the city," she said. Her father said nothing, but her mother turned away.

In her room, Dinah could see over the trees as the moon sank into the lake horizon, its long, sparkling tail disappearing into the dark water, leaving as the only light the bright, artificial glow from across the lake.

Withdrawal

Sunday

The soft tap of rain on the window. Cold rain. Cold room. Empty echoes: sighs, clink of glasses, rustle of sheets. I lie in bed, only sheetrock and shingles between me and the rain. Shaking, wrapped in pajamas, socks, robe, quilt, memories. I need heat. I need warmth. I need—I need—I need...I stare at the watermarks on the white ceiling from when the roof leaked—yellow whorls, like pee trails in the snow.

God, I hate Sundays. I hated them even before Marcie left. Days lacking form, lacking focus, now lacking love. Sleet pelting windows, tracks of rain shadows striating the walls, single wine glass on the nightstand, old wine and new dust dulling the crystal, like cataracts on lusterless eyes, lustless eyes, lustrous eyes like stars. Billions and billions of stars. Catch a falling star and put it in your pocket...Damn neighbor's playing Perry Como again. My sight strains, but the stars recede, fading to dots. Dots of light. Dots of stubble on my chin. Billions and billions of dots. Little raps at the door. Billions and billions of raps. A voice, sharp as the raps.

"Dan? C'mon, I know you're in there! I want my cat back, Dan!" Rap, rap, rap. The key clicks in the lock, followed by the futile rasp of the door pushing against the chair lodged under the knob. More rapping. Knocking. Pounding. "DAN! I'll be back!" Ignore, ignore. She'll be back. She'll be—

Sudden pain, sharp pain. Prickling on my skin, sharp jabs, tracks of iced needles: not needles, cat claws, the cat—

her cat—digging into my arm. Why in the hell did I steal her cat? I push the animal warmth away, returning the bed to an empty, cold sea, still smelling of her. No more crooked smile, half up, half down. No more stars. Gone like smoke, echoes within shadowed echoes. Dream of dreams, and bore of bores, Forever, and ever, Hallelujah!

I wrap the quilt around me and drag my shaking body out to the kitchen. On the counter is the wine bottle, half empty. Or is it half full? I eliminate the question. Now it's all empty. Like me. The landline phone shrieks and jars the air. Why do I still have a landline? The machine picks up. My buddy Todd's electronified voice booms through; Are you okay? Last night was a hoot. How's the cat? Come on out with us. Forget the bitch. He hangs up, and the machine sends a mournful beep into the ether. I press the "delete" button. Erase. Erase. Erase. From somewhere, a muffled "Ode to Joy" plays on my misplaced cell phone. I don't answer. There will be voice mail. Erase. Erase. Erase.

Monday

I call work and tell them I'm not coming in. Hell, that's what sick days are for. Sleep. Pee. Sleep. Feed the damn cat. Pain in the ass. What was I thinking? Sleep. The phone is beeping. I must have slept through the call. I check the message. Her voice shoots cold needles through me. *Come on, Dan, you made your point. Please return Orion. And come back to work.* I rewind and replay the voice message. *Come back to work.* I rewind. *Come back. Come back. Come back.*

I crawl back into bed. The cat leaps up next to me, and I push it off, ignoring its insulted meow. What the hell kind of name is Orion for a cat? The hunter. It shakes itself in a calico huff and disappears into the living room. I hear scratching—damn cat. I'll send Marcie the bill for a new chair. I think of the mouse droppings under the sink—the hunter. The only thing that fuzzball hunts for is the warmest spot in a room.

From my closet, the wire grins of empty hangers taunt me. A spot of pink glows from the floor. She had forgotten a cashmere sweater. I hold it to my nose, breathing her scent, then wrap its softness around my neck and go back to bed, where I lie still and breathe deeply, experiencing gravity weighing down on me, pressing on my chest. I imagine dying, my body caving in upon itself while my soul, pure and martyred, floats from my tortured body, moving up, up, out into the empyreal radiance. There's something Zen about imagining death. My soul arcs. It drifts further, over the city. Below, my spectral essence sights Marcie walking with her new guy. Poor bastard hasn't a clue. I float over and piss on her. Do souls piss? I jump up and dash into the bathroom.

Tuesday

I call in sick again and try to remember if I fed the damn cat last night. When I swing my legs out of bed to check, I step on the beast, and with a yowl, it rakes its claws across my ankle. Swearing, I limp into the bathroom to pour hydrogen peroxide on the scratches. I watch, fascinated, as hissing red froth rises from the scorched flesh, making my leg look foaming mad. I rip off some toilet paper and press it against the injury. The bleeding stops. At least on my leg.

The phone rings, and the machine picks up again. *Dan? Please come in! I need the specs for the Landry project. I won't fire you; I promise.* A laugh. Bitch. *And bring my cat with you!* Erase. Erase. Erase.

Phone again. Todd again: *Hey, Man, call me. I'm beginning to worry.* I text him: *I M OK.* But M I okay? I grab a box of crackers and limp back into bed. The cat flits up to the nightstand, teetering the wine glass, then launches onto the bed. It neither expects nor makes apologies for our earlier mutual infractions but settles against my unscathed leg. Its patchwork fur gleams in the stark gray light; its purrs vibrate against my bare skin.

Phone. Marcie. *Dan, this isn't funny. You'd better get back to work tomorrow. I need those specs. At least email them to me. I'll be by after work to pick up Orion.*

The rain has finally let up outside, but the wind is still thrusting obscenely against my windows, daring me to face its force. I feel some satisfaction at its impotence and fall asleep to its wailing rise and fall. The door buzzes. The chair scrapes. The voice curses. I rest my hand on soft fur to keep the cat from leaping off the bed and fall asleep smiling.

Wednesday

The bed smells less like Marcie and more like cat. My skin itches in pulse with the drip, drip, drip of the leaky shower. I scratch and consider the possibility of fleas, but it's probably just my filth—Marcie treated that damn feline like it was a sacred numen. The light in the room flickers in stop-action shadows as retreating clouds blow across the sun. I throw a wadded tissue to the cat, who bats it around. We are both enthralled. Then the cat rolls onto its back and begins gleefully shredding the tissue, leaving tiny white shards to mix with the cracker crumbs and bits of my heart scattered on the floor.

The phone. Todd: *Hey, I'm here whenever you want to talk.*

The phone. Marcie: *C'mon, Dan, please bring my cat back. I swear, I'm going to call the police! And when are you coming in to work? You're almost out of sick days. Damn it. I need those specs!*

I sift the cat litter in the bathroom box. The turds look like oatmeal cookies. I toss them in the toilet and flush. The cat jumps up on the bowl rim and watches, hypnotized by the swirling water. I refrain from the unreasonable urge to kick the beast into the bowl. Substitutes just aren't that satisfying.

My stomach demands food, and I order a pizza. While I'm waiting for it, I eat half a jar of peanut butter with a spoon. The cat jumps on the counter and tries to get its nose into the jar. I push him to the floor.

"You want food? Get the mouse."

Great. Now I'm talking to a cat.

Thursday

The sky is clear, brilliant. I lie, watching the sunlight move across my bed. I place my foot just ahead of the slanted rays and try to discern the movement of light across flesh until my foot is completely encased in the sun, warm up to my ankle. The cat pads onto my chest, and I rub his head. He arches against my hand, throat thrumming its warm little engine sounds. I amble into the living room, turn on the TV, where I stare at some show with a family tearing each other apart, screaming and hitting as the MC tries to separate them. I feel pleasant voyeurism watching someone more miserable than I. There's a sudden commotion in the kitchen—the cat must have gotten into the trash. Then the cameraman on the show gets tangled up in the fracas, and I laugh out loud, forgetting about the cat and possible chaos.

The cat dashes in. He has a dead mouse in his mouth and drops it expectantly at my feet. I exclaim my surprise, praising him loudly and petting him with one hand while grabbing a tissue with the other. I scoop up the mutilated remains and drop them in the garbage. Then I wash my hands, open a can of tuna and dump it in his bowl.

"Nice work, Orion," I say. "You earned your reward." He ignores me, delicately licking the mouse guts from his paws before approaching his bowl.

Knock at the door, replaced by insistent pounding. "Dan, if you don't let me in, I'm going to have Nick here break it down." I hold my breath. There's silence. Then a man's voice. "C'mon, Newman, give her the damn cat!" I watch the cat, fascinated by its fastidious table manners. Their voices get softer. "Maybe he's just not home, Marcie. C'mon, Babe. We'll get your cat later." They go. I breathe.

Who the hell is Nick?

Friday

I'm out of sick days. I can't lose this job, so I drag into work and hide in my cubicle. Mitch, in the next workstation, peeks around the corner. "Are you growing a beard?"

I growl something unintelligible, and he ducks back into his sterile coop. I stare at my computer screen—the inevitable approaches with the familiar click of stiletto heels on tile. Damn, you'd think she'd fall off those things, maybe break an ankle. I steel myself and fantasize about scaling the cubicle wall in a single bound. Nope, I forgot my cape. I'm trapped.

Marcie comes in bearing a cup of coffee, which she offers like an olive branch. At first, I think she is as beautiful as I remember, but I notice a tiny zit just below the corner of her lip. The imperfection is somehow comforting, and I'm able to keep from shattering into a pile at her feet.

"Truce?" She holds out the cup, which is only half-full. Or is that half-empty? It's cloudy with little lumps of undissolved powdered creamer. I take it black.

"You look awful. Are you eating?" she asks. As if she cared. I glare at her, not speaking. "You know, I do care about you."

"Right." Great comeback.

"C'mon, Dan, you know it would never have worked. And we weren't together all that long."

Her words jolt me. "Just long enough to have a litter box in my bathroom. Long enough to have your own drawer and space in my closet."

"We've been through this, Dan. I refuse to fight anymore."

I just keep staring at her. She looks whole, unscathed, unloving. Hadn't this meant anything to her? Where is her beard?

She sighs. "I want my cat back."

"I ate it."

She twists her mouth into disdain, half up, half down. "Grow up," she says. "And get those specs on my desk by noon." She turns to go, throwing back, "Nice chin fuzz."

I dump the coffee and get my own, black with two sugars, then play computer solitaire the rest of the day. Screw the specs. If she fires me, I'll claim sexual harassment.

Saturday

My beard prickles. Everything itches. I strip off my t-shirt and pajama bottoms and throw them on the floor. Then I get a wrench and fix the leak in the shower. The toilet rim is dotted with flecks of crud. I wipe around the rim with a tissue and pour in some toilet cleaner. The shelf by the sink is cluttered with a bunch of small jars and bottles: almond scrub, aloe cream, herbal pore cleaner, mango conditioner. A goddam spa—all sample-sized, I note. Was she also sampling me?

The shower turns on with a sputter, then courses, warm and steamy. I lean into the beating stream, letting the water pour down my face, chest, and legs, where the scratches have faded to pinkish streaks. I gradually turn the faucet toward the "hot" side, making my skin flush wine red, as I start to sing: *I am the egg man. I am the egg man. I am the lobster—Goo-goo g'joob.* I rub the green striped soap into my hair. Lather. Rinse. Repeat. The soap grinds on my face, shredding against the chin bristle. A pink Lady Bic razor is sitting on the side of the tub. Oh, hell, whatever. I grab it and carefully scrape my face fuzz, miraculously avoiding cutting myself. Water trickles along the cleared paths as little hair dashes swirl around and down the drain.

There's a call on my machine. It's Marcie: *C'mon, Dan, I'm pleading. Please bring Orion back.* I never noticed the edge in her voice before. Whiny bitch. The message continues—she must have forgotten to shut off the phone. A man's voice—the same one that was at my door—calls out. *Hey, Babe, you want to go out* (movement, shuffling)—*or stay in?* Giggling, muffled voices, then the phone clicks off. I stare at it while Orion wraps around my bare ankles.

The night is brilliant, with a full moon flowing across my bed. Orion's white splotches gleam as though under a black light as he curls against my leg, nuzzling the healing scratches. I accept his apology.

Sunday

My robe smells like an old basement. The bedroom has a dense reek of sweat, despair, and inadequate housekeeping. I strip the bed, then use a towel to wipe around the bathroom and toss it into the pile of robe, pajamas, and bedding. I drop the pink cashmere sweater on top and throw the whole thing into the washer, turning the dial to "hot." The machine chugs in a bouncy rhythm as I collect empty pizza boxes and grungy glasses and pour the old wine, thinner than blood, into the sink. I make myself a couple of hot dogs for lunch and toss a piece to Orion, which he bats about before devouring, like a caveman reenacting the big hunt. After transferring the wash load into the dryer, I go into the bathroom and sweep all Marcie's beauty crap into a shopping bag, along with the razor, still dotted with my stubble. I take the litter box, too.

My cell rings, and I retrieve it from under a sofa cushion; it's Todd, and I click it on.

"God, you're still alive! Christ, enough's enough already! You want to join the living?"

"What'd you have in mind?"

"We could watch the game tonight at The Keg. There have been some fine ladies around lately. You need to get back up on the horse. So to speak."

"So to speak," I say. The cat is rubbing against my leg. "I don't think I'm ready to go down that road again yet. But I'll meet you for a beer. Later. I got an errand to do first."

I'll take it slow. Someday I'll find someone whose smile curves up on both sides. The dryer buzzes, and I pull out the hot pile, find the pink scrap and toss it into the shopping bag, emptying the litter box on top. Then I scoop up the cat and nuzzle him to impart the scent of my aftershave on his fur. Let Marcie have a memory, too.

"Let's get going, pal," I say. Cradling the cat, I grab the shopping bag and my keys and head out.

Heredity

Lane stared at the door. He had traveled 2,200 miles across a 26-year gulch, and now only a one-inch door stood between him and his goal—a thin wooden divide that seemed somehow the most challenging obstacle to get past. His protruding Adam's apple bobbed up and down as he gulped down the sudden rock in his gullet. The sun scorched his uncovered head, and his wool Robert Hall sport jacket, fine for Waxhaw, North Carolina, was uncomfortably warm for the Las Vegas desert. His thin hair was plastered with sweat to his forehead, and his leg ached. He wondered if the heat would pierce to the metal pin that held his bones together, heating it enough to sear his muscles from the inside, and idly considered if he would feel it if it did. He'd never liked the thought of something so unnatural inside of him.

Other than that contemplation, the heat didn't bother him—he'd endured worse in the war, what with that oppressive jungle humidity. Hell, he thought, he should have worn his uniform, his medals—at least the purple heart. Even now, nine years later, it still resonated with people. As he reached up to knock, he winced at the sight of his lanky wrist extending slightly too far out of the sleeve. Karen had bought the jacket for him. There had been no extra longs, but the store was closing, and the jacket was on sale. This whole trip had been her idea. She had sobbed, begging him to do it, to make an effort to save their son. Remembering the purpose of the visit, he felt suddenly devious and considered leaving, forgetting the whole thing, finding another way to get a kidney for Jamie.

He fingered the small box in his pocket. So much was riding on the cheap gift inside. It had been his father's idea, and he hoped that the old man's memory was still accurate after all these years. Then, summoning learned courage, he took a deep breath, jerked his knuckles to the door, and rapped sharply with a forced authority. He counted four breaths before a woman opened the door, and for the first time in twenty-six years, he faced his mother.

She was not what he had expected.

Whatever phantom had floated in his mind, she was not it. All he had to go on were his hazy baby memory and some photographs as blurry as his expectations. Somehow, he had imagined her to look—not like this: an average, middle-aged woman with fluffy brown hair streaked with silver, a body beginning to surrender to gravity, and a face reflecting time and weather. He stared at her, considering how to start, the chill air seeping through the open door cooling his face even as the desert heat slow-stewed his body.

The woman shaded her eyes, looking up at the tall, thin man before her. Odd, there was something about him that seemed somehow familiar. He must have been near thirty, but he looked somehow younger in his poorly-fitting jacket and obvious discomfort. "Yes?" she said with an amused half-smile. "Can I help you?"

Lane faltered. Any scenarios of the reunion he might have imagined fled from reality. He waited for some rush of feeling, some warmth for this woman he had so long waited for, anticipating the return that never happened. There was nothing. All he felt was the desire to get this done, to save his son.

"Young man?" Her voice was calm and low, with a musical lilt. "Are you looking for someone?" He seemed so ill at ease, and she was amused and intrigued. She had always appreciated the surprises life offered and waited to see how this one played out.

He nodded, wishing that he could be glib, could swagger in, and say, "Yeah, I'm looking for my mama. Seen her in the past twenty-six years?" Then she'd look at him, and her eyes would suddenly glow with memory, then cloud over with tears. "Lane!" she'd cry, "My baby!" And she'd be his salvation. Or at least possibly his son's.

But he wasn't glib, never had been. Karen declared he was every woman's dream—a man who didn't talk and really listened. She loved to tell people how she had been the one who proposed, that if she'd waited for him to speak up, they'd be in an old folks' home before they got married. It was she who had insisted he make this trip to save their son.

The woman shrugged—probably an evangelist or maybe a first-time salesman. "Well, if there's nothing—" the woman started back inside when panic forced his words, and he shoved his foot between the closing door and the frame.

"Ma'am," he choked out. "You are Laurette Jackson, aren't you?"

The woman looked at him suspiciously through the narrowed opening. "Yes, I am. Do I know you?"

"My name's Lane Boudreau." Her face froze. "Your son." He mentally kicked himself for the lame addition.

"Lane." It was a breath rather than a word, and she wondered for a brief moment if this was a con. She examined his face for some familiarity, but it had been too long. "How do I know you're—him?"

"I got my birth certificate here," he said and reached inside his jacket, pulling out a folded piece of paper.

She looked at the unopened paper, then up to the boy's eyes, hazel with gold flecks, like Jim's, and was overcome with sudden disorientation, a sense of déjà vu, as though a dream had pursued her and appeared in the flesh. She opened the door wider, still staring at the young man as though he were an apparition.

"No, that's okay," she said, still reeling, her voice small. "I believe you. I always wondered when—if..." She jerked as though suddenly remembering her manners and adopted a more formal attitude. "Please, come in."

Just like that. Like it was the most natural thing in the world to open the door on your past, to invite it in for tea and cookies. He stepped in.

The desert heat that had enveloped his body dissipated in the cool of the foyer. An air conditioner somewhere hummed, and he felt his breath escape, steaming from hot lungs into the cooler air.

She led him into the house, trying to collect her thoughts. She had always wondered if this moment would come, how she would handle it. She'd made up the scenario in her mind, how she'd greet him and tell him about when he was a baby. Now that the moment was here, though, she was dazed by the surreality of it, and her mouth was dry as the desert outside her door.

"You probably need a drink," she was saying. "You drink bourbon like your daddy?" Lane thought, *so much for the tea and cookies.* He was surprised she could be so cool. The woman had no heart, that was for sure. *Well,* he thought grimly, *all I need is her kidney.* The thought made him smile—macabre humor. Karen always scolded him for it, saying it was inappropriate, but it had gotten him through the hell of war, and he needed it right now, in this new battle.

"Sure, thanks," he said, secretly looking around. The house looked normal enough, like any other desert abode: arched doorways, adobe walls painted a bright terra cotta and turquoise, tile floors, lots of big plants. Some paintings lined the wall: bold, bright desert scenes, vibrant sunsets, rundown huts.

Lane also noticed some paintings of waifs with huge eyes—the only pictures of children to be seen. There were no pictures of him or Tori anywhere, but he hadn't expected any. Why would she keep a reminder of the children she could so easily ditch? No other kids either, he noted. There was no surprise there, but he did realize a slight sense of relief he didn't quite understand.

She watched him look around as she poured out two glasses and handed one to him. Her nails were short and neatly manicured, her hands small, the tendons branching across the backs like the tines of a garden cultivator. He noticed her hands were trembling and wondered if it was from the moment or some medical problem. He hoped it was the former—he needed her to be healthy. She was his last chance. He needed her kidney to save his son's life, and he had to swallow any rage he might feel at seeing her. He was a good parent, even if she hadn't been, especially since she hadn't been.

"So. Lane," she said, and he automatically snapped into his army posture. He'd often found the straightness fooled people into thinking he was more confident than he felt. She appraised him over her drink. "Why now?"

Right to the point. He shrugged, trying to sound offhand. "Isn't it about time?"

She took a big slug of the liquor. She didn't usually drink so early in the day, but at this moment, she needed it. "Well, if you think so. Frankly, I'm a little surprised."

"That I could find you?"

"Lord, no. I kept no secrets. You daddy's always known where I was."

She wondered what he expected of her. Should she hug him? He's a stranger, after all. But oddly, she wanted to hug him, to connect in some way, reach across the years. She'd done the right thing in leaving, of that she had never doubted. He and his sister had a better life than they would have had with her. But that didn't mean it didn't hurt, hadn't haunted her. Her voice softened. "I'm just surprised that you wanted to find me. After all."

Her candor charged through him like lightning through a tree. There was no remorse, no shame from a mother who'd fled, leaving behind two babies. Yet, he felt no anger. Her attitude, her distance, would make this whole thing easier. He relaxed his posture and took a step toward her.

"Of course, I'd want to find you. You're my mother." He pulled the small flat box out of his pocket. "In fact, I brought you a present." He handed her the little box.

She opened the lid and pulled out a little bracelet. "Oh, my!"

"It's made of seashells. From the coast. Daddy said you always liked the shore."

She felt a rush of memories she'd long since squelched: running along the beach with Jim, holding Lane as he squealed in delight at the ocean waves. Baby arms around her neck, soft baby breath against her cheek.

"I don't know what to say, Lane." She slipped the bracelet onto her wrist and ran a finger over the shell ridges. "Thank you." She cleared her throat. "What about Vicki? How's she?"

"Her name's Tori."

"I always called her Vicki."

"Always? She was only a year when you—" He checked himself. He didn't want to start a fight. He couldn't afford to alienate her.

"She likes being called Tori better. She's fine. Married and living in Roanoke." He thought a moment and took another drink, giving a surreptitious glance over the rim of his glass. She was admiring the bracelet, and seeing her unearned happiness, he couldn't resist saying, "I asked her to come with me, but she didn't want to." She flinched slightly, and he immediately regretted the dig.

"Oh." She swirled her drink a moment, absorbed in the way the liquid sheeted down the side of the glass. "Can't say I blame her. It's a long trip."

He put down his glass. "All right, so tell me about yourself."

She took a sip. "What do you want to know?"

He considered. What could he say that would sound like he was sincerely interested? He wasn't above buttering her up to get her to give up her kidney, but he frankly wished he could get it done faster. He finally settled on the obvious. "So, what do you do?"

"I'm a singer." Her lips twitched into a bit of a smile. "Sort of. They call me a chanteuse. I sing at a nice little lounge down on the Strip. I do all right." A silence fell, and she nervously swirled her drink. She hated silence. After a moment, she had an idea, not maternal, but convenient. "You must be hungry. Let me make you a sandwich." She jumped up and went into the kitchen. Making him a sandwich would give her time to think. He seemed to be more polite than interested, so why would he find her after all this time?

Lane stood and walked around the room, relieved at the respite. He was surprised by the pleasant, everyday surroundings. He had expected her to be living in misery, just recompense for her unspeakable crime. Or maybe someplace decorated like a brothel, perhaps even a brothel itself, but not this average-looking room, clean, tastefully furnished. The landscapes on the walls appeared to be original artworks. He examined one closely and noted the artist's name scribbled in the corner.

"Verne did those," the woman said, entering with a plate holding a lopsided turkey sandwich, which she offered to Lane. "He's my—hell, I'm too old to say 'boyfriend.'" We've lived together twelve years."

Lane nodded. No commitment there, either. "I don't know anything about art," he said around a mouthful of turkey.

"They're good," she said. "Verne's well-known around here. He owns a gallery just off the Strip and does very well."

Lane nodded and sat to finish eating. He was a little disappointed to see what a nice little life she had. For some reason, he had hoped to find her wallowing in filth and guilt, her life destroyed by the dirt she'd dealt him and Tori and their father—although their father had never complained or said anything negative about the woman who left him. And their lives had not been bad at all. They'd grown up in a warm, loving home, eventually welcoming in the stepmother who had dried their tears and cheered their successes.

She refilled her glass and observed him, pondering the ache she felt, a feeling that had popped up intermittently, unexpectedly through the years. It would come at silly times, like during a TV show or commercial where a family was laughing and enjoying each other, and she'd feel a sudden swelling in her chest or a sting in her eyes. No, the years had not been without self-recrimination. And now that reproof had appeared on her doorstep and was sitting on her couch.

Lane finally swallowed the last of the sandwich. "Thanks. That was good." She reached out to take his plate, and he held her wrist, not tight, but enough to prevent her from pulling away. He was filling up with unwanted emotion, and it was time to pull out the big guns, get that kidney and get away.

"Are you happy?"

She looked away. "Can't answer that without bringing up the past," she said, and he released her wrist. "I guess you want to know how I could do it, huh? How I could up and leave two babies."

"We managed." He looked straight at her. "At first, we were just confused. At least I was. Tori was too little to understand. I just couldn't figure why Mama didn't come home."

He realized how nasty that sounded and quickly tried to cover it. "I mean, I was just a little kid. How could I understand what you were going through?"

"Listen, Lane, I was confused, too. I married your daddy when I was just 17, and you were born a year later. I was no mother, and I didn't know what to do with you. And then Vic—Tori came along. I'd always been kind of a wild child—I ran away with your daddy against my daddy's wishes. But marriage wasn't what I thought it would be. Oh, your daddy was good to me, but I felt—I wanted to sing, go to Nashville, get on the Grand Ole Opry. I just wanted to try. When your daddy let me go, I think he realized I wouldn't be back. I guess I realized it too, but I knew he'd take care of you." She turned away from him. "I heard he remarried."

Lane nodded. "He did. Donna. She's a good stepmama. A good step-grandmama."

The woman nodded.

He needed to move this forward. "So, you didn't answer. Are you happy?"

"Who knows what happiness is? I get to sing, and people applaud, and Verne and I, we have laughs. I guess I'm content."

"Do you regret—" he broke off. He hadn't meant to ask. He hadn't meant to care.

"Leaving you?" She shook her head. "Look at you, so tall and strong. You've done all right, haven't you?"

"You haven't asked anything about me," he said.

"I guess I figured you'd tell me anything you wanted me to know." She worried about getting into this, afraid it was someplace she couldn't escape. But it was open now, and she couldn't just ignore it. She forced a bright smile. "So, tell me all about Lane Boudreau."

He fumbled in his pocket for his wallet, rifling through it for a photo. "I'm married," he said. "Eight years, to Karen." He held out the picture, and she looked, not taking it.

"Pretty girl," she said. "Doesn't mind your limp?"

The words startled him—people usually didn't mention that.

"She knows how I got it," he said, waiting for her to ask. When she didn't, he continued. "In the war," he couldn't help a tone of superiority. "I'm decorated."

"Oh," she said, surprised. "I didn't know. You must have been very brave. You know, your daddy fought in World War II. He must be so proud of you."

She wanted to say she was proud, too, but felt she had no right. Damn, she didn't want to think about what else she had missed.

He pulled out another photo. "This is our son, James Rodney. He's seven."

She reached out this time and took the picture. "Named after his granddaddy," she said, examining the photo.

Lane nodded. "He's a good granddaddy." He couldn't resist adding, "He was a good father." She flinched slightly.

"I knew he would be," she said softly, then looked directly at Lane. "That's how come I could leave," she said.

Her admission surprised him, and he struggled to maintain his purpose in coming. He indicated the photograph again.

"I think he has your eyes," he said, adding, "now I see you."

She held the photo up a moment longer. "You think so? Maybe..."

"Oh, yes," Lane said, his head bobbing up and down. "Definitely."

"Well, what do you know? James Rodney, huh?" She seemed suddenly vulnerable, and Lane took aim.

"He's sick."

She looked up from the photo. "What do you mean? Got a cold or something?"

"No, really sick. He could die."

"My God, what's wrong with him?"

"He was born early, and he's had all kinds of troubles, but now he's really bad. His kidneys don't work anymore. They hook him up to a machine that washes his blood every few days. It's awful—he's so small, and he's such a good little soldier, just lying there, never crying." Lane gulped down hard. "Sometimes, I think it'd be easier on us all if he did cry."

"Awful. Isn't there anything they can do?"

"Well, sure, they can give him a new kidney, but they're pretty dear." Me'n Karen, we were tested right away. Daddy and Tori, too, but none of ours will work." He looked down, hoping he looked pitiful. "Even Donna got tested." She flinched. Direct hit. Then: "Kin works best."

He stole a sideways glance at her to see how she was digesting the news. Her eyes were wide and wet, her mouth shaped like a little "O."

He played his ace. "Mama?"

A shock shot through her.

The bastard.

"I see," she said, her voice a thin steel rod. "Yes, indeed, I do see."

"You're the only one left."

"You think I owe you, so you came to collect your pound of flesh." Her laugh was brittle. "Shakespeare, you know. I'm not so dumb."

"Please. To save his life. Look, at least get tested to see if you're a match."

She shook her head. "For what? As you've hinted, I was no kind of mother. What made you think I'd be a better grandmother?"

"Please, Mama—"

She turned away. He had appeared from the mists and unearthed all those feelings she'd successfully tamped down, and now he was twisting her around, trying to wring the last bit out of her heart. He didn't want her, just her kidney. An ache of disappointment became the scorching pain of betrayal, and she lashed out.

"Stop calling me that. I haven't been your mama your whole life. No sense starting now. You come here all sweet with your bracelet and your 'Mama,' and your pretending to care, and all you want is what you want."

Anger replaced hope. He said, "I'll do anything to save my son. That's what a real parent does."

She looked at him steadily. "Something I wouldn't know, would I?" She stood up. "You'd better go."

"What kind of woman are you? You don't give a damn about anyone else, as long as you get what you want."

She looked down at her wrist, then slipped the bracelet off and handed it to him.

"Like mother, like son, I guess."

His mouth worked, but no words came out. Then, facing a defeat he'd never imagined, a loss greater than the physical, he turned and walked out into the blazing Nevada sun as she watched him go, two people once united only by blood, now also sharing the burning agony of the loss of a child, one probable, one certain.

Plainsong

Tansy steps up to the microphone, and the world shifts into slow motion. Behind her, the band pulsates big brass, booming beat, and howling saxophones like foreplay. Before her, the shadowy movement of caliginous figures, backlit to opacity, a murky mob breathing as though one, daring her to entertain with the melodies stored in her throat and heart, perversely seeking the pleasure to be derived from her anticipated failure to enthrall.

The mic's silver orb becomes her focus. Its aura is a tight dome that pulls at her breath, sucking the notes from her depths, the rushing air inverting her diaphragm and pulling the sound up, up, to swirl around cranial cavities and burst forth through teeth and lips, an ethereal sound alternately eructing and crooning, spewing words and caressing tones. Her throaty growl transforms static notes into plaintive mating moans, black-widow sex-cries that end with an ecstatic, satiated death.

The audience reacts with an awed hush as her melodies tease and torment their ears, song after song, notes of pain and despair and rapture, the sounds of centuries wrenching from each listener a personal purification, delving into emotions unrealized and unexplainable. It's more than music: it's an exorcism, a purging, a catharsis. Tansy is more than a singer: she's a gypsy, an oracle, a prophet.

There is no patter between songs. She has nothing trivial to say, and they don't expect it; talk is not what they came for. Tansy lets the songs flow, one into the other, building and probing, presenting a theoretical picture of the artist, the illusion of a life beyond the songs, a peek into her depths, without a word of explanation or apology.

The spell continues, song after song, for just over an hour. Then, as her last blue notes hang, achromatizing into the air, the listeners erupt, salvos of cheers washing over her to shake her out of her sonant trance.

With a tiny tremor, Tansy awakens from her catalepsy and manages a smile in acknowledgment of the adulation being heaped upon her. She is exhausted, her breath, now freed from the demands of pitch, coming fast as though to catch up to the melodies that have escaped. She stretches an arm to acknowledge the musicians behind her, then waves to the still-cheering masses. Weaving slightly, she makes her way backstage where her assistant, Petey, stands ready with a glass of water and a towel, which he tosses around her sweat-drenched neck.

The theater manager appears from the shadows.

"How about an encore, Tansy?"

She shakes her head and manages a wry grin. "Leave 'em wanting more, right?" At his scowl, she pats his cheek. "I'm sorry, Grant, I'm wiped. You want me good in the second show, don't you?" There's enough magic left in her aura to soothe his avidity.

Back in her dressing room, she wriggles out of the heavy, sequined gown and hands it to Petey to air out, then envelops herself into a soft robe and collapses into a chair before the mirror. The music continues in her head; it's never completely gone, drumbeats connecting the synapses between neurons, dendrites transmitting weird harmonies throughout her brain.

"You were spectacular tonight, Babe," Petey says, moving behind her to loosen her ebony hair and gently brush out the spray and product as she watches in the mirror. She is alarmed at the faint streaks of silver.

"I was short," she says. "Grant wanted me to do an encore."

"You were fine," Petey assures her. "An hour is enough. No cabaret singer does more. And you don't take an intermission."

"I want to give them their money's worth."

Petey snorts. "Most come just to say they've been here," he snarls. "Rich folks who want to feel connected to their roots, who wants to feel the pain of poverty and abuse without the actual pain. The ones who really appreciate your music can't afford your shows."

He's right, and she knows it, but the comment is unnerving. The music in her head slows down and becomes Gospel, simultaneously filling her spaces, drawing her up and pulling her down.

It is interrupted by Dexter, who comes swooping in, his vast bulk filling the room, his bravado sucking the oxygen out.

"Well, Dexter the Ex-ter," Petey simpers, eyeing the big man appreciatively.

The hulk doesn't miss a beat. "Petey the Sweetie," he retorts. "Get me a beer, will you, doll baby?"

Petey catches Tansy's eye, and she nods, so with an audible huff, he heads out to the lounge. As she turns to her soon-to-be-ex-husband, her tempo picks up to match her pulse. Damn, the man could still rattle her.

"What do you want, Dex?"

The big man's face turns serious. "I'm still your husband Tansy..."

"Not for long. Your decision."

"...and we still have a daughter together. And she's in trouble."

Tansy turns, alarmed. "What do you mean? What kind of trouble?"

Dexter starts to pace, his face twisted in pain. "Drugs. Our baby's doin' drugs."

Tansy relaxes. The music slows. "That's it? A little pot? She's sixteen, Dex. Didn't you try it when you were a kid? Hell, don't you do it now?"

He stops pacing and glares at her. "I found needles."

Tansy's blood chills, turning her limbs to ice. The music grows louder, off-key. She can't think, can't speak through the cacophony.

"I found the shit in her room."

The noise builds, drowning out all thought. She lands on an idea. "I'll talk to her."

"Hell, you think that'll stop her? She's a junkie!"

"Where is she now? You didn't leave her alone?"

"She's in the car, out cold—Marvin's with her. I just stopped to tell you I'm checking her into rehab. Now."

"Wait, I'll go with you."

His laugh comes out a snort. "Like hell, you will. You got a second show to do. You never cut a show for anything. Don't worry. She won't even notice you're not there." The lowest blow, but she ignores the barb, focusing on the words second show. The music swells.

"She'll fight you."

"Hell, I'll tie her down and sit on her if I have to."

She nods. "Call me later. I'll go see her tomorrow."

He hesitates, a sharp retort at his tongue, but he swallows it. She sees the hesitation, knows without knowing what he is thinking as he turns to go. Cold, unfeeling. The words he said in the lawyer's office. He doesn't understand all the heat she expends in her music, how it drains, exhausts her.

"We all got our drugs!" she yells after him.

His big back stiffens, and for a moment, she wants to reach out to touch him, to hold him, to be the family he wants. But she doesn't, and without turning, he slams out.

The music crescendos, overpowering, and she sinks into a chair as Petey comes back in.

"You, okay? You want this?" he asks, indicating the beer in his hand.

Tansy shakes her head no. She is already running through her set in her mind, analyzing melodies, changing phrasing. She signals Petey to come help with her hair.

We all got our drugs.

The second show, she'll give them an encore.

The Gift

My family's pretty much like any other. We have relatives we brag about (like my great-uncle Willard, who invented vitamin-enriched lip balm) and those we just love no matter what (like my uncle Leonard, who went into business as a landscaper with the unfortunate slogan, "No grass grows under our feet"). However, we Sayers have one unusual characteristic: the Gift of Fate. Folks in my family can often tell the day they're going to die—and sometimes others' final days as well.

It's been a recognized family talent as far back as Emmett Parkinson Sayer, who fought with Tennessee's "Overmountain Men" in the Revolutionary War. On the eve of the battle at King's Mountain, he wrote to his wife that the next day would be his last and that she should sell the cows and go live with her parents. Of course, some might argue that he knew he was going into battle and could very well be killed, but see, he didn't die in the fighting. It seems later that evening, he wandered off to pee, and in the darkness, stumbled into a trench and broke his neck. Anyway, that's the first documented incidence of the Gift. Many more followed, and as the pattern developed, the Gift became a recognized fact of Sayer-dom.

Oh, sure, there were times the circumstances have been a little suspect. For example, when my great-great-great-grandfather, Andrew Johnson Sayer (for whom I am named), declared his imminent demise one spring morning and was struck dead that very afternoon by a bolt of lightning, some might have questioned why he was in that tree sawing a branch during a rainstorm. Still, most just figured it was Fate that made him do it.

Then there was my mama's cousin, Lemuel Sayer Townsend, who choked on a peach pit. Now, he hadn't told anyone he was going to die on that particular day, and there was some rumble about how maybe the Gift had weakened through a diluted lineage (we don't all marry our cousins), but then his mama, my great-aunt Lucy, produced a letter she claimed Lem had written that very morning, saying it just hadn't been noticed in all the commotion, what with him dying and all. It said:

> *Dearest Mama—Today will be my last. It is painful to say goodbye, so I will simply say you have been the finest of mothers, and I will be proud to meet you someday in Heaven. Please feed Elvis [his dog].*
>
> *Love, your son,*
> *Lemuel Jackson Sayer*

There, Lucy declared, in his very own hand, was proof Lem had known he was going to meet his maker that day.

And there are other instances, each dutifully and wholly recorded in the family Bible right next to the date of death. As the legend goes, the honoree may know when he'll meet his maker, he just doesn't know how, keeping the Gift—and the Giftee—from assuming a God-like aura.

The McMahons, my daddy's family, do not have the Gift, nor do they want it. Daddy has already told Mama he does not want to know her final "when." He doesn't want folks thinking he treated her any differently because he knew she was closing. (Daddy's in real estate.) Nor does he want her, if she gets the notion, telling him when to shine his shoes and aim them skyward, saying he'd rather be surprised, thank you. My younger (by ten months) brother, Will, and I do not yet know if the Gift has passed on to us. We've discussed it and decided we'd rather be caught unaware, so we don't have to chaw on it for any discernible length of time.

But let me get to the meat of this story. See, Grandpa Sayer had moved in with us, lock, stock, and running shorts, better than seven years ago, after Grandma died. From the first, whenever Will and I said goodnight to Grandpa, he'd give us each a hug and say, "You boys are my legacy. Always make me proud." It made us want to be better than we were like we could someday be men worthy of the name Sayer (even though technically we were McMahons).

After Grandpa retired as a doctor two years ago, he continued to check on some of his old patients, including Kate and Remus Cantrell. They own the Chicken Shack down on Jefferson (a stop usually planned for around lunchtime). Then there's old Miss Jeanette Boudreau in the Shady Lane Retirement Home and Gunner Reeves, who shacks up with Miss Sadie Lowry in her neat little trailer behind the IGA. (Mama always said God would lay waste to Miss Sadie's sin-wagon with a tornado someday, and—but that's another story.)

This particular Wednesday, it being the first day of summer vacation, my inamorata, Nan, and I were in the kitchen planning our summer: working when we had to, swimming in the backyard pool, driving down to Sparta to bowl, and seriously fooling around whenever possible.

Mama runs a graphics business in Cookeville, two doors down from Daddy's office, and in the summers, they've taken to popping home for lunch, supposedly for Will's cooking. We suspect it's just to let us know that we better toe the line even though it's summer vacation. That day, Will was country-frying steak and green tomatoes when Grandpa came back from his "rounds." He was on the porch, talking into his cell phone in his usual loud voice (he's a little deaf and tends to speak louder than he knows).

"That's right, Saturday night is the dying time," he said. He might as well have been saying the dog needed a bath, but the way it sounded, I felt an icy hand squeeze my heart like a tube of fake cheese. I glanced around the kitchen and saw everyone else had a deer-in-the-headlights look. We heard the phone close with a snap, and Grandpa came in. He didn't seem to notice us all sitting there staring, and after a moment, he shook his head a little as if to clear it.

"I'm going for a run." That's all he said to us, but his voice was low and sad sounding.

Mama went up to him and hugged him.

"Oh, Pa," she said.

At first, he didn't seem to understand, but then his face lit up with comprehension.

"Lily—"

She interrupted him. "I'll call the kin so they can all be here."

He looked at her a moment like his wheels were turning, then nodded and went up to change, leaving us all to digest the impact of his overheard proclamation. After a moment, Mama, always the most practical, being a Sayer and all, thanked Will for a delicious lunch (it had burned to inedible during our catatonic reaction), went into the bathroom, and ran the water hard for a good ten minutes, then came out with red-rimmed eyes and pulled out her address book.

"We can figure for the laying-out on Sunday, so everyone's here," she said, her voice sounding like it was full of peanut butter.

The following two days felt all messed up, like one of those weird paintings of melting clocks. Will said it felt like he had a heavy sack on his back, and every time I looked at Grandpa my throat filled with the words that were stuck, thick and hot as boiled-down jam ready to pour into jars. I wanted to say something, but what—stay with me, don't leave, never die?

At first, Grandpa avoided all the hubbub, but the second day I caught him watching Mama make her special chocolate funeral bundt cake. He nodded.

"Funeral cake," he said. "Seems right."

He swiped a fingerful of batter and smiled at her, which set her crying again. He looked on a minute, his face full of sad, then turned and went out. As we prepared, we never talked to him about the Grand Inevitable, and although he had a melancholy settled about him, he never said anything about it either. Mama kept us so busy getting ready for the expected influx of family that we didn't talk much, but every so often, in passing, we'd stop and look at each other, tears filling but not spilling, and then we'd move on.

"There'll be time for crying later," Mama said. Every so often, Daddy would touch her arm or give her a quick hug, which for Daddy said more than another man sinking to the floor and rending his garment. At night I'd lie in bed and listen to the faucet running full force in my mother's bathroom while my own heart felt clogged as a drain full of hair.

Whenever Grandpa was out, as he was more frequently now, I noticed his doctor bag was also missing. I thought about all the stuff he had in there for pain, and I wondered if and how and where he was using it. Thinking about it while polishing a spoon, I rubbed so hard I went right through the silver overlay to the dull metal beneath.

On Friday afternoon, I caught Grandpa coming back from a run looking fit to go another fifty years. I tried to imagine that strong heart stilled, then shunted the idea to the back of my brain to be strangled by evasion.

"Grandpa," I said, hoping my words didn't quiver. "Tell me it's not the Gift."

"Andy—" he replied. He cleared his throat and looked like he wanted to say something, but just then, Mama came in.

"That was Aunt Dolly on the phone. Imagine, she and Uncle Henry are going to drive all night from Charleston to be here. Andy, I need your help in the garage."

Grandpa looked from Mama to me, then sighed. "Yes, Andy, it's the Gift." He tilted his head to indicate I should go, and that was that.

The family began arriving early Saturday morning. Being just over in Wilson County, Aunt Lydia was first with her clan, bringing in big batches of cornbread. "Mmm, mmm, lookin' fine, Lyddie," Grandpa said, appreciating the contents of her fancy glass pans. "You know it's my favorite." Aunt Lydia busted out in a bawl, and Grandpa patted her back and suggested she lie down after her trip. He picked up his bag to go out again, and I tried to follow him, I don't know what for—to talk, to hug him—but was stopped by Uncle Fred, who thrust a huge pot of navy beans at me with the order to "rinse 'em, sort 'em, and soak 'em for later."

The whole day was like that, with relatives trotting in from all over and me being shoved and ordered about till I was dizzy. Uncle Henry Sayer and Aunt Dolly arrived from Charleston a bit disheveled, having driven their house-sized RV all night just to be on time to say goodbye. They brought their four kids, a watermelon, a cooler of fried chicken, and a big bucket of fresh sweet cherries, which Aunt Dolly explained were for the pies she intended to make because she knew how Grandpa loved her pies. She settled right into the kitchen, pulling out pans and ingredients and making a lot more noise than was probably necessary. Then Aunt LuAnn arrived with Uncle Big Jack Kincaid in another major camper, toting a gallon bucket of potato salad and several jars of her state fair pickles. The men compared miles traveled and Uncle Henry, who won, went out back to claim the hammock and sleep off the drive.

And still they came in SUVs and campers, whooping and calling out and reminding me of the Mongol hordes we'd studied in Western Civ. The Memphis Sayers got in around eleven, and by afternoon we saw license plates from North Carolina, West Virginia, and Mississippi. Cousins I hadn't seen in a hawk's age showed up, and we older kids swapped tales while the little ones splashed in the pool or ran around with the dogs, chasing Frisbees, squirrels, anything that moved. People filled every corner of the house and lawn, chatting, laughing, telling, and re-telling the old family stories.

"Lord," Nan whispered to me. "You'd think your family never saw each other!"

"We don't get together much," I admitted, washed in a powerful sadness as to the reason for the current assemblage.

As the day went on, the food for the wake piled up. Mama and Daddy sent Will and me around to the neighbors to borrow cots and blow-up beds for everyone, as they'd all be staying over for the funeral. (Our family doesn't believe in a long laying-out. As my great-grandma Sayer used to say, "Just stick me in the ground, eat the funeral vittles, and get on with the living.")

Our big house was nigh to busting, voices tumbling out onto the wide back lawn where kids ran on into the evening, swimming, catching fireflies, and rolling around with the dogs. We kept the local pizza delivery place busy and made an occasional run to the Chicken Shack; anyone passing by would've thought it was a party, not preparation for a final farewell.

At last, unable to stand the crowd any longer, I slipped away, down to the little creek that trickles through the woods behind our yard, where I went whenever I was filled with teen angst. I considered how silly all those other pains had been when compared with the big empty feeling growing in my chest.

I was only a little surprised to see Will already there—we often thought the same. He turned to see me coming, then whipped back, and I saw him quick wipe his arm across his face. I sat next to him, saying, "Hey."

"Hey," he echoed. No more was needed, and we sat there watching the water burble along on its way to something bigger than we'd ever considered before.

Thinking it was time Grandpa should be home, we picked up and went back to the house, now a veritable Sayer family convention. Grandpa was there all right, working the crowd, back-slapping, swapping stories, swinging the little ones high above his lanky frame. I watched him, a heaviness filling me from tip to toe. I needed to talk to him alone, but I figured everyone else needed him, too, so I just watched and caught Will doing the same. I caught the occasional mournful look, or a tear brushed aside, yet they were few and quickly sequestered, replaced by a funny story or a hug. I would have thought this a sensible way to approach the unavoidable, except that it was Grandpa, and I couldn't make myself sensible.

Once, my cousin Merle nudged me and said, "He don't look much like he's in dyin' mode, does he?"

"You disputin' the Gift?" asked Merle's brother, Jackson, and the two started whaling away at each other, rolling around like they'd done ever since they were little. I admired

Merle's defense of the Gift and wished I didn't have the sick feeling he was right. After all, Grandpa had declared it, so how could I dispute?

Grandpa went in for a nap about mid-afternoon, and a hush fell over the place. We all wondered if this was it, and I desperately wanted to run after him, to beg him to come back. But would that be right? He seemed pretty O.K. with the whole thing; could I deny him a dignified exit by my unchecked begging and wailing?

When Grandpa emerged after an hour looking refreshed and more alive than ever, I felt a stirring of hope until Will whispered, "He did say Saturday night." I would've punched my brother for stealing my hope had I not known he was hurting as bad as me.

"Look at him," Nan nudged me as we sat munching pizza in the deepening dusk. There he was, the nearly departed, sitting on the big porch swing with a group of little Sayer cousins grouped around, bug-eyed at some fantastic story he was weaving. I'd heard every one of those stories, and I missed them already, even as I thought of all the future missing-hims I'd have.

We'd all have those times of emptiness, I knew, whenever we stopped running long enough. As I walked through the amassed throng with similar noses and kindred eyes, I could almost feel the thread of our heritage in the familiar stories that wafted about, and a lit coal began to smolder in my gut. I wanted more stories from Grandpa, wanted them to go on and on. He should be there to set my children on his knee and tell them about Emmett Parkinson

Sayer, Cousin Lem, and all the other old stories that drew us together against the cold. That was what I wanted, and the fact that it was to be taken away from me just as I discovered it was an insult to me and an affront to my lineage.

I was stewing about the cruelty of the situation when I noticed that Grandpa was nowhere around. I felt my panic rising as I feared that he would go without me saying something, anything, everything that needed to be said. I skirted the citronella candles and crossed the wide yard, scanning the crowd, and finally saw him way off to the side, in the willow shadows. The moon had risen full-blown, and in the penumbra, he looked prematurely apparitional, his white hair and shirt luminous. I took a deep breath to tamp down the fire within me, then sidled up to him and stood there, not speaking, not knowing what to say.

"Our whole family," he said, breaking the silence. "Did you ever see such a crazy bunch?" He shook his head and laughed.

The fire inside me flared, and the words spilled out in a rush, true as rain.

"I don't want you to die."

He looked surprised. Then his forehead wrinkled up in thought. "Andrew, at your age, death's just a concept, not a reality. You were too young to—well, appreciate your grandma's death. But you've got to realize that everybody's going to die. I'll die. So will your mama and your daddy and everyone here, though God willing not for a long time."

"I know, but..."

"And when it's time, it's time, and there's nothing we can do about it."

"But when you're gone, who's going to take me hunting? Who'll I run with? I want you to see me go to medical school, see me be a doctor like you."

He looked pleased. "You want to be a doctor?"

He was surprised! It hadn't occurred to me that I had never told him before, that I had just assumed he knew. I wondered what else I had taken for granted.

"Well," he said, sounding like he was talking around a mouthful of cornbread. "Well," he repeated, softer. "Listen, boy, I have to tell you—" He stopped and thought for a moment, then cleared his throat. "Andrew," he said finally. "I will see you, no matter what. I'll always be there with you." He draped an arm around my shoulders, and it surprised me that our eyes were on a level. "After all," he said, "I have to keep an eye on my legacy." The familiar words warmed and sent a shiver through me all at the same time. I nodded, not trusting my voice. Together, shoulder to shoulder, we made our way back to the family.

It was way late by now, and everyone had arrived. We'd all chowed down, and the little ones were drooping on their daddies' shoulders, reaching sleepy arms out to grab at fireflies or stars.

At last, Grandpa stepped up on the porch and stretched.

"Well, it's late. Guess I'll turn in," he said. The mood suddenly grew sober.

"Goodnight, Pa," Mama said, hugging him tenderly. "I love you."

There was a hush as, one by one, the family walked by him, giving him a hug or a kiss or, in the case of Uncle Henry, a vigorous handshake and a shoulder pat. As I hugged him, he held me a moment longer.

"I'll be seeing you," he whispered, and I nodded mutely and moved over so Will and Nan could hug him. Then I watched him go in, and I prayed, but nothing came back except an unspoken "No."

We bedded the littler kids down in the two RVs while the adults who hadn't scored a bed either by age or infirmity searched out soft spots to lay their various bones. Displaced from our rooms, Will and I joined Nan and the cousins on blow-up water rafts on the pool deck. We all lay in the dim glow of solar lights, mumbling now and again, our eyes heavy with sleep as the house lights winked out one by one.

I stared a long time at my grandpa's dark window and finally fell asleep cursing the Gift. I wished I didn't know about it now, and I prayed I hadn't inherited the damn thing. I never wanted to know when I was going to die.

In the light of morning, the tone was appropriately somber as everyone woke and gathered on the lawn waiting for Ma to come down with the sad, certain news so the real purpose of the get-together could commence. Finally, she came out the back door, looking sort of vague. We all stared at her, holding our collective breath.

"He's gone," she said, her voice sounding kind of surprised. You could hear everyone exhale.

"Well, I guess we'd better call--" Aunt Lydia began, but Ma stopped her.

"No, I mean, he's really gone! He's not here!"

Everyone gawked at her like a big old herd of Holsteins chewing their cuds. You could see people's minds working behind their vacant stares.

"Praise the Lord. He's risen!" Bertha suddenly burst out in a fit of the rapture, but Daddy patted her shoulder.

"James is a good man, Bertha, but I hardly think— "

"Well, where in hell is he?" asked Uncle Henry, effectively spanning the entire Kingdom. "We drove four hundred miles for this!"

"And I truly do appreciate it," Grandpa's voice called out, followed by his actual, nondead being, jogging around the corner of the house.

"Pa?" My mother sat down hard on the porch step.

"Hey, he ain't dead!" shouted my little cousin Toby, as proud of his discovery as the kid who saw the emperor's nakedness.

"No shit, Sherlock." His older brother, Punk, smacked him across the head.

"Thought I'd get in an early run," Grandpa said, as though it explained anything. Everyone stood in stunned silence, watching him sweat.

"Hey, Grandpa," Will said, a weird little grin creeping across his face. "Glad you could make it for breakfast."

"But—Pa, you said—the Gift—" Aunt Lydia stuttered.

"I didn't say anything. You all figured on your own. But I must say, it's sure nice to have everybody together." He looked right at me, as ashamed as a hound dog who'd lost his rabbit and mouthed one word: "Sorry."

There was a shocked silence. I felt a knife of white-hot anger creeping up from inside and slicing through the knot of sadness in my chest. He had known all along, and hadn't told me, had allowed me, allowed all of us to suffer! What kind of twisted joke was that? I looked around at my family, gaping open-mouthed, a group of nonstop talkers suddenly shocked into silence.

Uncle Henry was the first to speak, his voice strangled with suppressed rage.

"What the hell, James! I drove four hundred miles—"

A few others then burst their dams, too, some shouting, some crying, some just slamming their hands on tables or chairs. And there in the midst of it stood Grandpa, alive and prepared to be so for years yet to come, healthy, vibrant, the sweat of life darkening the front of his T-shirt. And I saw his face crumble from a smile, darkening into something more akin to extreme annoyance.

"Well, Goddamit, Henry," he exploded. "I am SO sorry I inconvenienced you by not dying! Next time I'll be sure to oblige!"

And suddenly, as I looked at my grandfather standing there, not dead, my anger fled, replaced by a joy I'd never known before. I started to laugh.

I couldn't help it, and I couldn't stop. I don't know if it was the tension of the past few days or just my goldurn happiness that Grandpa wasn't dead, but I laughed so hard I had to sit down."

"And what's so damn funny to you?" Uncle Big Jack growled.

I had trouble getting the words around the laughter. "You—you're all pissed that he didn't die! That he's alive and well!"

There was another silence, and then Will joined Nan and me, and suddenly everyone was laughing, and people started running up and hugging Grandpa and each other. The air was filled with joy and life that vibrated up to the heavens where I swear, even God was laughing at these damn fools He created.

Well, we had ourselves a fine party that day, what with all the food everyone had brought. And Grandpa was smiling and asking, "How many people get to see their own wake?" We all talked and ate and hugged and laughed, and it felt real good. Aunt Lydia fluttered around Grandpa, filling his plate with cornbread whenever it was empty, and Mama just walked around, kind of dazed. Henry and Dolly finally had to take off because, as Henry kept reminding us, they had four hundred miles to go, causing Daddy to suggest they get the award for "most miles traveled." Before they left, though, Henry suggested we do it again in a month or two—at their house this time—and everyone promised we would, barring any unforeseen events—like death.

Finally, everyone was gone, and the brightness of the day was fading once more into blued shadows, leaving a fading pink-gold line poking holes through the trees. Will, Nan, and I were sitting on the edge of the pool dangling our feet in the warm water while Grandpa, Daddy, and Mama were stretched out on lounge chairs, marinating in the weekend's memories. We were laughing at some of the stories we'd heard when the phone rang, and Mama went in to answer it.

"D'you think Grandpa really will know when he's going to die?" Will said in a low voice. "Or any of us?"

"Depends. Do you believe in the Gift?" I asked.

"I do," Nan piped up. "But not necessarily the gift you mean. Imagine—all those people dropped everything to come and say goodbye. That someone can be so loved, that's the true gift." I stared at her. That's one of the things I love about Nan—she's so deep. That and her dimples. We were chawing on that thought when Mama came out, visibly shaken.

"That was Martha Hart," she said. "Seems Miss Jeanette Boudreau died in her bed last night." She looked at Grandpa. "She had her will and all her official papers all laid out on her nightstand, along with directions for her funeral." Mama's voice softened. "Martha said she had never seen such peace on a person's face."

We all stared at Grandpa, who leaned back in his chair. He closed his eyes and nodded, heaving a long, sad sigh that seemed to deflate his body. And as I looked at him, then at Mama and Daddy and Will, I felt a sudden surge of joy. I knew right then that the Gift was real but that it didn't matter if I had inherited it or not. Either way, the Gift was just one more connection, a spider strand in a web that tied us all to whatever was before and to whatever would be after.

The Mikvah

Minucha Kagan's world was one of absolutes. In a greater world where the very temperature change of the planet was subject to debate and dissension, where a celebrity's smile and his attorney's artfully crafted arguments could sway a jury even in the light of irrefutable evidence, where television and the Internet supplied new trends to be discarded like pistachio shells, where nothing was certain except that nothing was certain, the Kagan household followed the law of the Talmud much as it had been followed for thousands of years.

Outside, the world shifted as often as the truncated spellings of a text message. Within Minucha's home, communication was less capricious, where the Word of God mingled with that of her father, a man of great love but of equally great conviction, who loomed at a level only slightly below Moses. With the fervor of another age, he prayed for his sons to follow in his footsteps as an attorney and for his daughters to someday be wives, mothers of children, bound to a man deemed proper in a life strictly prescribed by tradition. Among others in the Orthodox circle, mothers were teachers, doctors, realtors, but within the *eruv* of the Kagan home, the division between women and men was a *mechitzah* as clear as the physical divider in the synagogue.

But while the level of autocracy was perhaps extreme, the Kagan home was by no means an austere throwback. Education was encouraged, even for the girls—at least to the point where it didn't interfere with their home duties. After all, Mr. Kagan explained, a woman should be able to intelligently converse with her husband, and Minucha often heard her parents discussing politics or other worldly concerns, her mother kneading the challah while her father sat at the kitchen table with a cup of coffee. Two large televisions and several computers brought the world into the Kagan home, with educational video games encouraged, as were music lessons on piano, violin, guitar, cello, and clarinet, the family orchestra growing with each additional child.

As the eldest of what would eventually be nine children, Minucha accepted this tenet as her lot, that everything was God's will; she had no reason to question such a dictate. Still, sometimes Minucha wished she could, like the music, float through the windows and spread herself out on the wind.

When she heard her father, in his morning prayers, thanking God for not making him a woman, a small tickle fluttered in her mind, and Minucha began to wonder at the sarcasm of a God who could see her as inferior. She could run faster, throw a ball farther, and swing across the playground equipment quicker than the red-headed Weinberg brothers who lived next door. She loved whirling about on the various climbing bars, her dark hair flying free, her skirts flapping open to the clear Chicago air.

Then one day in the park when she was eight, her mother stopped her. "Minnie, no more climbing."

"But why, Mama? It's fun!"

"You're getting older, *kotchkala*, and it's not right for a girl to show her underpants. No roughhousing with the boys and no more climbing."

Minucha later complained to her brother, Nossi, who was eleven months younger than her. They were sitting in the room Nossi shared with their twin brothers Velvyl and Shyah, taking turns practicing the little Suzuki violin they shared.

"It's not fair!" she pouted, pensively plucking at the strings. Then she had an idea.

"I could climb if I was wearing pants."

"Girls aren't supposed to wear boys' clothes," Nossi said.

Minucha considered. "Men only wear a tallis in shul," she said. "Maybe it's the same thing for pants on girls."

Nossi considered, then pulled a pair of black pants from his dresser drawer. "Okay, you can wear mine."

Minucha grabbed the pants and ran into her room to try them on. She was slender, and Nossi was a tall boy—a *langer loksh*, their mother called him—and the pants fit her fine. She tucked her blouse into the waist and ran out to join her friends, enjoying the foreign feel of the fabric between her legs.

She was hanging by her knees from the top of the climbing bars when she saw her upside-down father striding across the grass toward her.

Before she could right herself, he helped her off the bars, setting her down on the pea gravel layered around the equipment.

"Minnie, you disobeyed your mother. Look at you, wearing men's clothes!"

"Nossi's not a man," she pouted. Then, emboldened by the smile she saw crinkling her father's mouth, she went on. "He's a little boy. Littler than me."

"Hey, Lazar, you've got a live one there!" laughed Mr. Weinberg, who was watching the children play. Her father stood up and sighed.

"She's smart," he said. "Maybe too smart. A real lawyer's mind." He turned to Minucha and patted her cheek. "*Vilde chayala*. Let's go home so you can change."

"Papa," she said, trotting along to keep up with his long stride. "What if you bought me girl pants? Pink ones? My friends wear them. They're not boys' clothes."

His eyes were wide but amused.

"And I thought I was the litigator in the family!" He shook his head. "Let others wear them. You're my daughter, and you'll follow my rules."

She was quiet a moment, thinking, then said, "Papa? What's a 'lawyer's mind'?"

"Huh. You hear everything too, don't you?" He thought a moment. "A lawyer's mind can twist ideas around and find the hidden reasons behind things," he explained. "It's a way of thinking to make facts say what you want them to say."

"A lawyer's mind," she repeated softly, liking the way it sounded. So be it—she would be a lawyer. At night, alone in her bed, her little sisters breathing the untroubled sleep of ungendered dreams, she would think up ways she might circumvent the rigid rules placed upon her lowly female self.

◆

The family owned a cottage on Plum Lake in Wisconsin, and weekends were often spent running in the grass or sand and splashing happily under their mother's watchful eye. Evenings, they read or played their instruments, two pastimes that transcended gender as they gave concerts for each other or discussed Torah and various secular books.

Minucha had always been free to swim with her brothers and sisters, splashing together in the cold, clear water, baking to a tan as they floated on large black inner tubes or the flat wooden raft. The summer she turned eleven, her father stopped her from running into the water with Yossi.

"You're a woman now, my Minnie," he said, and she blushed, knowing that he was referring to the fact that she had recently begun menstruating. "You shouldn't swim with men anymore. It's not decent."

She watched as Yossi and her other siblings laughed and splashed. "That's not fair," she pouted. "I want to swim, too."

"You can swim with your mother and sisters when the boys come in," he said. "We'll set up a schedule. Right now, just stay on the shore."

Her disappointment blocked her sense of propriety, and she blurted out, "What about people on the other side of the lake? When we swim, there could be men swimming there that we don't know about."

Her father smiled. "Ah, that lawyer's mind," he said, considering her argument. "Good, good, but if that's your argument, I would have to say then you can't swim unless we're sure no one is in the water. And how would we know that? You wouldn't be able to swim at all. Now, what do you say?"

She considered her recourse. "I'll follow the schedule." She turned away, hiding her disappointment. "Excuse me," she said archly. "I'm going to read. Off by myself. Where no one can see." She turned and walked off in what she hoped was a huff.

Each summer after that, she rankled at the unfairness of the rule. When her sister Chani "entered womanhood" too, she joined Minucha on the beach, waiting for the boys to decide to come out. Now and then, the boys would torment their sisters by lingering in the water beyond their allotted time, daring the girls to come and make them get out.

Once when she was fourteen, after being denied a swim for most of the day by her brothers, Minucha decided to take her turn whenever she could—even at night. Her parents had admonished the children against swimming alone, and breaking that rule compounded the thrill of darkness as she tiptoed out of the cabin and crept to the water. The moon was full, and the sky bright. Staying within the shallows bounded by the raft, she floated, enjoying the soft warmth of the water caressing her air-chilled skin.

Above her, pinpoints of stars appeared between lazy clouds with moon-silvered edges. Staring up, Minucha saw in the moon what was surely the face of God. He was smiling at her, and she smiled back at the apparent approval of her deception. There were ways to get around the rules, she thought. One only needed to use a lawyer's mind.

After that, she chose her arguments carefully, waiting to speak until she was sure she had covered all her bases. At sixteen, she suggested to her father that she needed a job. He'd been working in his den, and at her request, he turned away from the computer.

"I could buy my own clothes," she said, adding, "and I'll give half my salary for tzedakah." She knew he would not resist a charity appeal.

"It's a fine idea, but you would have to be off on Shabbos and holidays."

She was ready for this. "All set. I'm in Bloomingdale's children's department, and I work Sundays and after school. No Fridays or Saturdays."

Her father stared at her, then shrugged. "Okay, Emma Goldman. You win."

◆

The job was liberating, made all the more so by one of the girls she worked with. Julia was also Jewish, but her family was not Orthodox. She was sassy and funny, and Minucha envied her both her casual relationship with her parents and her freedom. One airy spring day, they sat eating their lunch on a bench in the mall courtyard. Next to the trendy, miniskirted Julia, she felt dowdy in her brown sweater set and long denim skirt.

As they ate, a young man wearing tight jeans and a t-shirt crossed the mall, and Julia openly admired his lazy gait. He saw her and flashed a toothy smile.

"Mmmm," Julia said around her mouthful of tuna sandwich. "Look at that tush. I wouldn't mind walking behind that!"

Minucha was shocked, but she laughed. "Is that all you think about?"

"Well, yeah. Don't you? God, don't you ever wonder about sex? I mean, your mom had nine children. Your folks must really burn up that bedroom."

Minucha almost choked on her chopped liver sandwich, the idea of her parents being carried away by passion at once horrifying and amusing.

◆

During Minucha's senior year at the Jewish Day School, talk naturally turned to college. Minucha had secretly applied to several schools and had been accepted at all of them. Now, acceptance packets in hand and arguments at the ready, she prepared to face her father. With a deep breath, she strode into his den and set the packets on his desk. He adjusted his glasses and looked at the pile.

"What's all this?"

"Acceptance packets. I want to go to college."

"Of course you do. You're a smart girl." He examined the packets.

"Wisconsin. Minnesota. Michigan." His eyebrows shot up, and he smiled. "Northwestern. The University of Chicago. Very impressive." She basked in the moment, knowing it would end with a but. She was right.

"But what for?" he said.

"Please." Her voice was low, a prayer. "Please."

He considered. "You really want this?" She nodded, afraid to speak. He set aside the packets from neighboring states. "These are too far," he said.

"What about Chicago? Or Northwestern? I could still live at home."

"Too expensive," he said. "I have your five brothers to educate." She noted he did not include her sisters. "What about the University of Illinois? The downtown campus has a fine Jewish studies program, and tuition is more reasonable. After all, you'll quit when you get married anyway."

Minucha banished the last words from her mind. She grabbed her small victory and would deal with the rest later. "That will be fine. Thank you." So what if it wasn't her first choice—she was going to college! And Jewish Studies wasn't an unusual major for a future law student.

She loved the campus and enjoyed her classes as a Jewish Studies major. Still, she often traveled to the University of Chicago, to the law school campus when she had time. There she wandered through the building or stood outside of the classrooms, breathing in what she hoped would be the air of her future.

One day in late May of Minucha's freshman year, she finished her last exam and decided to extend the warm day. She hopped the "El" and soon was sitting on a bench by the law school's large reflecting pool and fountains. Across the Midway Plaisance, on the wide grassy expanse, bagpipers were practicing for the upcoming graduation, and as she listened, she noticed a young man sitting on a bench nearby, his head bent over his books. He was dressed casually in a green sweater and jeans, but he wore a *kipah*. The yarmulke kept sliding off his curly copper hair as he read, and each time he automatically reached up and replaced it, as though it was such a part of him he didn't even have to break concentration.

On an impulse, Minucha looked in her purse and found a flat hair clip. She always carried several because "*kipah* control" was often a problem for her father and brothers. Shyly, she approached the young man.

"Excuse me," she said tentatively. He didn't seem to notice her, as he was so deep in his book, which she saw was a study of torts. She spoke louder. "Excuse me."

His head shot up, and the *kipah* went flying. As he grabbed for it, his book began to drop, and he twisted adroitly, one hand snatching the book before it hit the ground and the other snapping out to grab the *kipah* with effortless grace.

"I'm sorry," she said. "I just thought you might like this." She opened her palm with the clip, and the young man glanced at her. His eyes were clear, blue as Lake Michigan, and she felt a quickening below her stomach that made her legs quiver.

"Thank you," the young man said, his voice soft, musical, matching the breeze that strummed the blossoming trees. He secured the small yarmulke, which had a baseball embroidered on it along with the words, "Go Sox."

"I'm a Cubs fan myself," she said.

"Ah, then we must never speak again," he said, and his sudden smile stole her breath away. At that moment, the university carillon began to ring; the young man's head jolted around, but this time his yarmulke stayed firmly in place. "Thank you for the clip," he said, and ran off, leaving Minucha alone with the chimes.

She looked for him again each time she returned but never saw him, leaving her to revive and relive the encounter in her mind. It was enough to stir but not to sustain, and she was both happy and miserable in her restlessness. Sometimes she dreamed that blue eyes floated above her, dreamed of strong arms around her, and in her sleep she felt her heart beat faster, felt her back arch as her body was overtaken by a wave of sensation that broke, leaving her to wake spent, wondering at her own body's longings. She knew enough to realize what she had experienced and wondered if she should feel guilty about it while secretly longing each night for its return.

◆

That fall, she was at the den computer, filling out her online registration, when her father came in. He looked over her shoulder, and she steeled herself to continue as though he weren't there until he spoke.

"So, how long is this nonsense going to go on?"

"What nonsense?"

"I've set you up with several nice young men, but you've rejected them all."

"I'm not looking for a husband."

"You don't have to. I'll look. You just pick one."

"I want to be a lawyer," she said softly.

He looked troubled, and his words were sad. "A lawyer is not a good life for a religious woman. It's too time-intensive, leaving no time for your family. How would you make a good Jewish home?"

"Other Jewish women are lawyers. You have some in your office."

"They are not my daughter. Get married, make a home." He silenced her protest with a look, and she knew it was one argument she would not win.

That November, she was reading Rashi for one of her classes, curled up in the large leather chair in her father's den, when he came in and stood looking over her shoulder.

"There's a new young man in my office," he said. "He's coming to meet you Saturday night." While Minucha pondered the statement, he went to the bookshelves, pulled out a thick volume, and placed it on the table next to her chair. "Here, look at Rambaum's commentaries," he said. "You'll like the additions he makes."

As if I have a choice, she thought and reluctantly picked up the book.

On his way out, her father turned. "He's smart, this young man. He went to Chicago law, top of his class."

A sudden flutter in her stomach signified hope, and Minucha smiled into the Rambaum. The more she thought about it, the more she knew it had to be her red-haired student. *Mama always said God makes shidduchs,* she thought, so God had planned it. This was her reward for always obeying, even if reluctantly.

◆

He was here.

Minucha heard the bell, faintly heard the voices downstairs. She took a deep breath and tried to glide gracefully down the wide, dark-wood staircase. Her sisters Chani and Devorah were sitting on the landing bench giggling, and she gave them a cutting look. Their turn would come. Her father was at the foot of the stairs, talking to the young man who stood away from her view. Her heart beat faster.

"Ah, here she is now," her father said. The young man in the hallway stepped into view, and Minucha's smile froze.

The man looking up at her was a stranger—dark, with soft features and brown eyes. She stopped on the bottom step, and when he came up to her, he was barely taller than her. She quickly stepped down and looked at her father. Surely this was wrong. It was not the shidduch she knew God had meant for her.

"Min, this is Jacob Kaplan." She turned to the young man and smiled automatically, manners winning out over disappointment.

"Jacob. I'm glad to meet you."

He was smiling, not speaking. She couldn't tell if he was appraising her or just shy. Her father stood nearby, considering the considerer. Suddenly the suitor came to life.

"Oh. Here." He handed her a small bouquet of daisies he had been holding.

"Thank you," she said, thinking she would have preferred a good book. Her father went into his den.

"Well, shall we go?" Jacob took her coat from her arm and held it out for her.

"Alone?" She was surprised her father hadn't demanded a chaperone.

"I will do nothing but respect you." His look was mock-serious, and she found herself smiling, pleasantly surprised at his gentle teasing.

"That's good," she said. "I'd hate to have to hurt you."

He eschewed her suggestion of a movie, instead suggesting dinner at a kosher restaurant. "I'd rather talk," he said. He was obviously excited about the law, although as a first-year in her father's large office, he did little but write briefs and take depositions. She enjoyed his enthusiasm. Jacob spoke as though she were an equal, able to understand the intricacies of his torts and briefs. She, in turn, asked questions, and he patiently explained the answers.

He listened as she talked about music, a subject he claimed to know little about, and made her promise to go with him to a concert. More dates followed, and the months passed in easy camaraderie. He kept his promise about respecting her, although he did risk a kiss on their third date—a chaste, friendly kiss rather than one of passion. She enjoyed the kiss, and the many that followed, enjoyed the stirrings they evoked inside of her. Perhaps, even more, she enjoyed the fact that her father probably would not like the idea of her kissing a man that's not her husband. At least not yet. The more time they spent together, the more she felt comfortable with the possibility.

Still, in her dreams, she walked with a red-haired man, holding his hand, drawing close to him. And it was he of her dreams who caused her body to clench and then release, spent and calm. She held her guilt over this fact in check, enjoying the privacy and the rebellion of her secrecy.

◆

When Jacob proposed on Chanukah, she accepted, and they decided on a spring wedding before Passover. Life with him would be comfortable and friendly, if not exactly passion-filled. But she could find that passion in her private thoughts, feeling guilty at her deception, yet unable to refuse it.

After the ceremony, the newlyweds were swept away into a divided crowd, where they danced—she with the women, he with the men—then were seated in chairs and both hoisted high. A large white handkerchief was tossed up into the air to Jacob, who then flicked an end to her, and they "danced" without touching, laughing and bobbing like two leaves on a rippling lake.

Later, as she prepared for bed in the hotel suite, Minucha discovered that her often unreliable period had begun. Probably from the excitement, she reasoned. Well, so much for the wedding night. She came out of the bathroom to face her new husband, who waited, his face shining with drink and excitement. Embarrassed, she wordlessly held up the box of sanitary napkins. His face fell. By Jewish law, sex was not permitted during menstruation.

Jacob sighed and shrugged. "Well, we're not the first for this to happen. We're both tired anyway, so tonight we'll sleep."

Then he slipped into bed and placed a couple of pillows next to him, indicating that she should sleep on the other side. "To avoid temptation," he said. "It's okay, Minnie. I can wait."

His words were both a reprieve and a disappointment. She wanted him to want her so much he couldn't wait. She wanted to want him that way, too, part of her wishing he would refuse to wait would tear off her nightgown and make her feel the excitement of her dreams for real. But he just sighed and turned over, and she slipped into her side of the bed, feeling sorry for him, but also, deep down, a bit relieved and confused by her feelings. She drifted off to the dream of red hair and blue eyes yet again and woke to the now-familiar shock of climax. Afterward, she lay awake a long time, considering that on the other side of the pillow divide lay her husband, unaware of his bride's solitary wedding night consummation.

◆

They moved into their new apartment the next day, postponing their honeymoon until after the upcoming Passover holiday.

"I'll have to get my hair cut off before Passover," she said that evening after dinner in their new kitchen. She was putting plates in the sink to wash, and Jacob came up behind her and curled his arms around her waist. He reached up and curled a dark strand of her hair around his finger.

"You don't have to cut it for me," Jacob said. "You don't have to keep it covered, either. At least not here at home." He buried his nose in her hair and pressed against her. "It's so beautiful, almost alive." His comments had surprised her as much as his touch. Until she attended the *mikvah*, she was a *niddah* and considered untouchable. But Jacob wasn't as strict about things as she would have guessed someone would be who was selected by her father, and she found his little breaches thrilling.

After her period ended, she counted the requisite seven days, then visited the small brick building that housed the *mikvah*. In the preparation room, Minucha showered and washed her hair, enjoying the feel of her thick wet hair against her neck and shoulders. It made *mikvah* a little more difficult, as she had to search for and remove loose hairs before going in and then had to be sure to dunk deep enough, so no hair floated above. Still, she felt her small rebellion was definitely a triumph.

After showering, she sat at the mirrored dressing table and trimmed her toenails, then filed her fingernails. Even short nails had to be filed slightly before going into the mikvah so that nothing should block the water from touching and purifying every little bit of skin. When she was completely clean, she wrapped herself in the thick robe left on the door and entered the immersion area.

Abbie Dubman, the women's overseer, greeted Minucha warmly and held the robe and towel as Minucha stepped down into the pool to where the water just skimmed the tops of her breasts. Minucha had visited the mikvah for the first time just before the wedding, so she knew what to do. Lifting her toes from the tiled pool floor, she dropped into a relaxed fetal position, opening her body, slightly parting her eyelids, her lips, spreading her fingers and toes to let the water cleanse every inch of skin. She floated a moment, hearing nothing but her heartbeat in her ears, feeling the swirl of her hair above her, the warm caress of the water. Then, when she could hold her breath no longer, she braced her feet against the floor and launched herself upward, breaking through to meet the air, exhilarated. She was a seal, a dolphin, and a mermaid, breaching the water to command two worlds.

Abbie handed Minucha the towel to cover her head while she recited the requisite prayers blessing God who purified through immersion. She dunked again, relishing the weightlessness and watery embrace, then reluctantly stepped up the stairs leading out of the water and took the robe.

Somewhat embarrassed by the older woman's knowing look, she went to prepare for her husband.

At home, Minucha paced nervously, knowing what Jacob would be expecting when he got home from work. Her stomach had been fluttering all day, and when she had the urge to use the toilet, she was surprised to see the blood in the bowl.

At the news, Jacob was nonplussed. "What? But you just had your period!"

"I know," Minucha blushed to be discussing such a personal matter with a man so barely her husband. "I-I've always been irregular...I'm sorry, Jacob, really, I am." She turned away from the disappointment in his eyes, surprised that she actually did feel a curl of disappointment along with slight cramps.

"Well, we have the rest of our lives together. I guess another couple of weeks won't kill us." He smiled wanly. "It'll only feel like death," he joked, and she felt genuinely sorry for him. He kissed her lightly, his lips lingering, and she again felt a thrill from his casual disregard of the purity laws.

Once more she counted the days, and this time found herself eager to go to the mikvah. She took her time in the preparation room, enjoying the soft music, the sweet-smelling soaps, the feeling of being pampered. Again when she immersed, floating in the warm water, she felt an indescribable joy.

She came home again feeling apprehension and also that familiar heaviness below her stomach. As Jacob entered the front door, she felt the blood begin once more and rushed to the bathroom. This time, however, Jacob turned pale when she told him. He was shocked, even a little suspicious.

"Min, it's normal to be nervous, but you don't have to be shy."

"Do you want proof?" she asked, surprised at her own boldness. His face colored and he apologized. Seeing his pained look, she cringed inside. "I know it's been difficult for you, Jacob—" she began, but he cut her off.

"You don't know!" His outburst startled her, and she turned away. His voice softened, and he turned her and drew her to him. "I'm sorry, I'm sorry, Min. I'm just worried that something might be wrong." He peered into her face, concerned. "Go see the doctor. Tomorrow. Please." She nodded. "Come on, you probably don't feel like cooking. Let's go out to dinner."

Her small sense of triumph at his acquiescence shamed her. He was her husband, after all, yet she couldn't shake the feeling that she had won something precious, that perhaps God was on her side after all, and she reveled in the belief that He was allowing her the delight of the mikvah without the ensuing obligation.

Her doctor said she was fine, that such happenings weren't unusual for young brides, and suggested some relaxation techniques. Time passed, and Minucha again counted the days to mikvah. She and Jacob had fallen into an easy, comfortable pattern, and chances were good that this time there would be no reprieve. Still, she felt somewhat cheated, wanting the passion she found in her dreams to be in her husband, who was so patient. Now, although she yearned for the freedom of the water, she disdained the certainty of the afterward. Suddenly, a thought struck her like a lightning bolt through her brain.

Jacob did not have to know she was going to mikvah.

The thought settled into her mind, the power of her realization struck her. It was her decision and hers alone, and no one would know but her. She also knew she was breaking the rules, those set down by God and her father, but she didn't care. How had God repaid her fealty in the past? Denied her both the possibility of law school and the blue-eyed man, laying both before her as temptations, then snatching both away.

The next morning, she told Jacob that she was unable to go to mikvah that day, that her unreliable period had come early. He sighed, but all he said was, "Well, as long as the doctor says you're all right. It'll be a story for our children. If we ever have any." He was joking, but his face betrayed his frustration. She felt a stab of guilt, yet the secret power within her remained, and she said no more.

She spent extra time in the preparation room, shaving, plucking, singing in the shower. Then, reciting the prayer, she let herself be welcomed by the warm water. As she bent her knees and dipped below the surface, she blew a little air out of her mouth and felt the water eddy, felt little bubbles of breath—her breath, her life—float to the top of the pool. As she surfaced, she felt a strength, a power she had never known, and she dunked once, twice more, reluctant to leave the womblike warmth. Afterward, she lingered in the preparation room, drying and brushing her hair until it gleamed, rubbing sweet lotion on her body and working it slowly into her legs, arms, chest, and face. There was a sensual pleasure to the motion, and she felt a pleasant stirring in her stomach, but it was not foretelling a period. They slept with the pillows once more between them that night, but her sleep was dreamless.

The next day was Friday, and Minucha labored all day, cleaning the small apartment until every surface shone, and by late afternoon the fragrant bouquet of roast chicken, sweet plum-and-apricot compote, pungent cholent, and fresh-baked challah all mixed together creating a promise of plenty. She was peeling potatoes and humming when she heard Jacob enter the front door.

"You're home early!" Minucha called cheerfully, wiping her hands on her apron. She wore a white kerchief holding back her thick hair. Her eyes sparkled, and her cheeks were rosy from cooking, but Jacob didn't smile or hug her.

He dragged heavily into the kitchen and dropped a small pastry box on the table. His voice was strained. "I stopped at the bakery on the way home and ran into Aaron Dubman. He gave me your ring." He dug into his pocket and tossed her ring on the counter. "Abbie had asked him to give to me if he saw me." He looked at her, his eyes dull. "You left it yesterday at the mikvah."

She froze a moment, and the silence hung on the air like a foul odor. The feel of the ring was still so new, she hadn't noticed its absence. She saw his face and turned away, biting her lip.

"Why did you say you were—? Why didn't you tell me?"

Her hands fluttered helplessly. She couldn't look at him. The truth came out before she could stop it—before she even knew what she was saying.

"I wasn't going for you."

She had expected rage, shouting, maybe even a slap, but she was not prepared for what happened next. He fell heavily into a chair and began to cry, loud, gasping sobs. Taken aback by this outburst, Minucha sat down across the table, her helpless hands flopping like fish, wanting to soothe him yet not daring to touch him. She should say something, she thought, but no words would form.

Finally, he raised his head and stared at her. His face was blotchy, his eyes red. "Who is he?"

Of course, she realized, he would think she was cheating on him.

"There is no 'he,'" she said. He looked at her, uncomprehending.

"No one else?" The thought settled behind his eyes, and his mouth twisted into a wry grin. "No one else, but not me. Why? Do I so repulse you?"

His tear-streaked face tore into her heart, and she felt the surprising tug of shame, of pity, no, of something more.

She struggled to explain. "Well, maybe there is someone else," she said. "Me. I did it for me."

Ask me why, she thought. Ask me what I am thinking, what I want, what I need.

"No one else," he said, the thought settling behind his eyes. He sat up straighter. "I understand, Min, I do. You're frightened." He stood up. "But you're my wife. Come. It's time."

He walked to the stairs without looking back. She stood for a moment, hesitating. Then, surrounded by the smells of home and Shabbos, she slowly followed him up the stairs.

He was surprisingly gentle, his kiss light at first, as though testing her, and she found she enjoyed the feelings that stirred within her. She was at first taken aback by the unfamiliar tap of his tongue against her lips but even more surprised by her unconscious opening to it. Her body yielded as well, her skin melting to the air until she floated, a mere wraith.

It was in that same dreamlike state that she was vaguely aware of him laying her down onto the bed, his hands carefully removing her clothing, his soft gasp before he lay on top of her. His heaviness was a pleasant weight that warmed her skin the length of her body. Then there was his careful prodding between her legs and the first quick, sharp pain. She involuntarily gasped, and he hesitated as though waiting for her to say something. When she remained silent, he continued moving, covering her face, her throat, her body with kisses, and she enjoyed the taste of his lips, the scent of his breath. As she gave herself up to a mounting excitement, she had the fuzzy awareness that the feelings of this reality were different from those that had churned her dreams. From some distant plateau, she heard him call her name, and as she clutched him with increasing need, she thought, felt, knew that her dream would never be the same.

Jacob was still sleeping when she slipped out of bed. She had tried to sleep, but there were no dreams, and she awoke with a slight ache between her legs from muscles newly used. Her mother had told her there would be some blood the first time, but there had been no blood. Still, she felt a desperate need for purification, but how? It was night now, and she padded downstairs. The supper lay drying in the uncovered pots, and she hadn't lit the Shabbos candles. There was a punishment for that, she thought, but she couldn't remember it. She lit the candles anyway, but the *brocha* wouldn't come. She needed purification first.

But it was Shabbos; the mikvah was closed.

All she needed was a free-flowing body of natural waters. Like a lake. Like Lake Michigan, a scant mile away. She dressed quickly and silently slipped out the door, walking east beneath the streetlights, oblivious to the foolishness of her quest.

The beach was glowing beneath the almost-full moon, nearly bright as day, and the water moved in small silver-tipped waves that lightly spanked the sand. She stood at the water's edge, drawn to the faint light along the horizon, wondering if it was dawn or just the lights of far-away Michigan glowing on the other side. Kicking off her shoes, she stepped in, expecting the shock of cold, but the water was satiny and warm. She wriggled her toes in the spongy mud, then pulled them out of the sucking ooze, letting the grains wash away. She stepped in deeper. The hem of her skirt, heavy with wetness, pulled the material downward, tugging at her hips like a lover eager to undress the object of his desire.

Yes, she thought, yes. She unbuttoned her skirt and let it fall, stepping out of the floating fabric, then walked in further, stripping off her underskirt and white cotton panties, stopping only to pull her legs through and then letting the clothing drift away. The water reached her waist, and she unbuttoned her blouse and pulled off her camisole, until at last, she was completely naked, the water slapping gently above her bobbing breasts. Untying the kerchief that imprisoned her hair, she set it on the water and shook her hair free. Then, releasing her feet, she pulled herself into a partial fetal position and dunked below the surface. The movement of the water played with her, pushing her back and forth, and she momentarily could not tell if she was up or down. She kicked around with her feet until she felt solid ground, then pushed upward, breaching high, laughing and tossing back her hair in a trailing arc of water beads. She looked for the kerchief and spied the white spot a little ways over. She swam to it, reveling in the free movement of her legs, the water swirling around her inner thighs, her breasts, her arms, her ears. The backward pull of the water against her hair thrilled her, and she dunked her head again, playing, making somersaults as she strained to feel the water encircling every strand, filling every opening.

Finally, she stood and after wringing out the kerchief, she placed it upon her head and spoke the prayer to God who has commanded that women perform the mitzvah of mikvah. Then she set the kerchief flat upon the water and watched it as it gently rolled out farther and farther, a little white boat seeking its shore.

Minucha felt the waves growing, the current pulling and pushing her body becoming more insistent, more demanding, as though the lake was tired of merely playing and wanted more of her. A large wave smacked her in the face, making her sputter. Shaking the water out of her eyes, she saw another, larger wave heading for her. For a brief moment, she panicked, then, thinking quickly, released her foothold and dipped below, rolling beneath the wave, jounced about by the increasingly insistent currents. She broke into the air, gasping and laughing, and saw she was beyond the wave, had escaped its pull. She could no longer find the lake floor and floated free, rising and falling with the swells.

Above her, pinpoints of stars could be seen between the scudding pearl-edged clouds. She floated as behind her the din of waves smashed their impotent anger against the shore. She had outwitted them, she thought, as she floated, serene. There was no fear, only peace, and Minucha stretched her opened body on the water, secure that she would be able to ride the waves back to shore whenever she so chose.

Release Point

Ruth took a deep breath and re-entered the overheated funeral home. The Wisconsin autumn was doing its usual quick-turn into winter, and she brushed a few random snowflakes from the thick brown hair that refused to stay in the clasp at her neck. "Free hair," James had called it, declaring it had a mind of its own as he smoothed it away from her eyes. She tried to remember her husband's touch now, to hold onto it, as if by remembering it she could feel it again.

She maneuvered past the coffin through the sea of dark suits and uniforms clustered around the easel displaying President Bush's mounted letter praising James's bravery in Iraq. She wished she could have stayed outside, breathing in the cold, fresh air, pretending she was anywhere else, somewhere with James and Casey. She closed her eyes and for a moment was back with them; the "unholy three," her mother had jokingly called them as they laughed their way through childhood and adolescence, to an adulthood that was more complicated than any of them had anticipated.

Someone touched her arm, and she opened her eyes. With a jolt, she remembered. James was there, lying in the flag-draped casket that dominated the room, attended by solemn-faced brother marines. She looked at the owner of the touch, Mrs. Kincaid, her old Sunday School teacher, who was saying something, her mouth drooping with sadness. The murmur of voices in the room, though respectfully low, was suffocating, and Ruth struggled to catch her words.

"...so sorry, dear. He was such a lovely boy and a brave man."

Ruth nodded. She had heard the same words so often during that long afternoon that they no longer registered any meaning. This wasn't supposed to be—at barely 25, she was a widow where, despite four years of marriage, she had never really been a wife.

Her plain black dress still carried the mix of cold air and cigarette smoke as she stepped beside James' mother, Grace, who claimed her hand, grasping it as a lifeline.

"Are you all right, Ruth?"

"Yes, Grace. Are you?"

"As all right as can be expected."

The older woman tilted her face upward to her daughter-in-law. The effect of gravity slightly smoothed her skin, giving it a delusional softness in sharp contrast to the heavy shadows rimming her eyes—James' bister eyes, brown irises with a slight grayish corona. Ruth scanned the room for her father-in-law.

"Where's Harold?"

Grace ran a veined hand through her gray-streaked hair. "In the back. They had a place where he could lie down. This has all but destroyed him." She sighed. "Men are weak."

"James wasn't weak," Ruth said.

Grace looked at her with eyes that knew more than was said. "Wasn't he?"

The question saddened Ruth. She knew how close James had been with his mother, how her newer pain only layered on that of the past. Despite the holes in her connection with

James, Ruth's own suffering was keen enough. She tried to imagine if she and James had had a child if she would have had that bond. But of course, that would never have happened. Still, she could imagine it, that wresting of the heart, and she wondered how Grace could still be standing there, calmly greeting people, accepting condolences. Heaviness lurched back into her chest, the wave swelling, cresting, and receding, leaving the constant nausea that had dominated her being ever since the visit by the stone-faced military contingent, just—could it be only weeks ago?

James had been the quintessential favorite son his entire life: Eagle Scout, high school football hero, church youth leader, college salutatorian, decorated Marine. Now all of Plum Grove had turned out to honor him. For five exhausting hours, Ruth, Grace, and Harold had hugged and shook hands and thanked countless blurred faces for coming: old friends, both male, and female, local politicians, and VFW representatives, former teachers, uniforms mixing with suits and jeans. Now the crowd was thinning; there would be more tomorrow morning, more hands to shake and shoulders to hug, then the service and the burial in the family plot, with all honors befitting a hero.

For a brief moment, Ruth's eyes skimmed the floral arrangements festooning the room with spots of bright color that would soon wither and die. Life's promise dangled like a carrot before a mule, then was yanked away while you skittered along, wondering where it all went, wondering if it had been there at all.

The casket was closed, the flag tucked carefully around it, as neatly as if it were merely a bed covering, and James, inside, merely sleeping in his dress blues. But there would be no pre-sleep chatter, no good-night kiss, only darkness. Fatigue pulled on Ruth's body, and she longed to rest, to crawl into the coffin next to James and sleep.

A woman approached—a bartender, Ruth remembered, at a place in the city James and Casey frequented. They had taken her with them a couple of times. She hugged Ruth and whispered, "I'm so sorry, Honey. He always spoke very highly of you. They both did."

She moved along, and Ruth mechanically accepted a long hug from one of the black suits, faintly placing the wearer as their insurance agent.

"He was a hero," the man intoned solemnly.

The words heard so often came off as inane, meaningless. Ruth's mouth smiled, and she nodded as he moved on to hug Grace, who had returned to Ruth's side. "I know how much pain you must be in," the man said before moving over to look at one of the poster boards plastered with photos of James throughout his life, many including Ruth and Casey, a cascade of facades.

"People always say they know," Grace whispered in Ruth's ear. "They don't know. They don't know anything."

"They know what they want to know," Ruth said.

Grace looked at Ruth, the sadness almost palpable. "Yes, I suppose that's true. You know, there's been talk about you and Casey."

Ruth looked evenly at the older woman, and an unwanted smile tugged at her lips. "Me and Casey."

"I know the truth. I always have. But it doesn't matter anymore, does it?"

Ruth had no desire to continue that conversation with her husband's mother. Her late husband's mother. She would have to get used to saying that. It was strange—it sounded so much more acceptable than ex-husband, yet she would give anything to be able to call James that, to know that he was still alive. This way, this late husband was wrong. At least the other way he would have been happy, even if it meant they weren't together. They would have still loved each other, however, that love manifested.

Ever since she'd received the news, she hadn't slept. Her mind wouldn't focus enough to accept any of what was happening around her. Now her body begged for a reprieve. She couldn't breathe, couldn't bear another hug, connecting at shoulders and arms only, don't get too close, don't hold on too tightly—poor widow, alone, unloved. Grace's words, *they don't know anything,* rang in her ears. She was drowning, had to go back outside, get some air. She worked her way through the crowded room, smiling wanly at condolences, shaking limp hands, nodding, holding it together, holding everything together, just as she had always done. Grabbing up her coat from the chair where she'd dropped it, she escaped outside.

The rush of cold air slapped her hot cheeks, and she wrapped her coat around her and circled the side of the mortuary to the little green area away from the parking lot. She wasn't surprised to see Casey there, hidden from the throng, huddled on a bench amongst the evergreen shrubbery. It's funny how for such a huge man, he seemed so tiny now, and his body curled tightly inward as though he were trying to crawl inside himself. His hair, always so carefully arranged, was a wild blond mess now, falling loosely across his broad forehead.

She reflexively reached out to brush a lock back, and he jerked up in surprise, looking at her blankly for a moment, pale eyes wild, unseeing. Then his face crumbled.

"My God, my God!" He enfolded her in a bear hug. Wrapped in his arms, arms that understood and knew, she felt safe and protected enough to let down her guard. Who cared if people saw or what they thought. Casey was the shelter she needed now, the only one who understood her grief and could draw it from her like a warm cloth draws out the frostbite. She sobbed, gasped, and wailed against his shoulder until, at last, spent, she calmed down to low hiccups. He handed her his neatly folded handkerchief, and she rubbed it across her eyes, inhaling the clean Casey scent.

She finished her tearful spasm, and they sat down, fingers interlaced, warm where they touched, backs icy against the frosty air, immersed in silence as a spray of snowflakes dotted their hair and coats. When Casey finally spoke, his voice was low.

"Ruth, I'm going to come out." He peered at her as though measuring her reaction as she struggled with the import of his statement.

"People will know—"

"It doesn't matter anymore, does it? And you gave up so much for him."

Ruth considered. What had she given up, really? James was the only man she had ever loved, and she had been willing to do anything to be with him. She recalled the late nights watching old movies and inventing new drinking games, remembered cooking with him, hiking with him, remembered the laughter.

"I had everything I wanted," she said.

"Ruth." Casey squeezed her hand, and the remembered laughter stopped as though frozen, then shattered into fragments of echoes.

It had always been the three of them—or the two of them without her. She remembered the tender glances and touches that weren't hers to claim, remembered James and Casey saying good-night to her and closing the bedroom door, remembered lying alone in her dark room across the hall.

She stared now over the brittle, snow-dusted lawn, past the crowded chapel parking lot, past the highway, to the frozen lake that lay beyond. She closed her eyes and was once again floating on that lake, lying on a big rubber raft, the warmth of the sun on her face and legs, James and Casey laughing as they splashed on either side of her, horsing around, dunking each other, tipping her into the water. They were kids then, the three of them always together, children in their own Eden before the apple was eaten. Before things got complicated. Before James decided to join the Marines; before he asked her to marry him and be his shield; before she, blinded by her love for him, agreed.

She opened her eyes. Casey was watching her. "I know this sounds terrible," he said, "but this frees us both."

"You know what it'll do," she said. "This town isn't forgiving. You can't do that to his memory. He deserves to be remembered the way he wanted." Her mind rushed for a handhold. "Look, Casey, we could get married. After a decent interval, I mean. It would make sense—we were all so close. No one would be surprised. We could keep James' memory intact, and we could just—go on."

Casey shook his head. "We already lived that lie." His smile was wan. "Ruth, you have to move on, find your real life. We both do."

"People will know—"

"So what? Will he be any less of a hero? James is dead, Ruth. You're alive."

"I loved him. I can't betray—"

"We did what he wanted. But he was selfish to demand it. Maybe it was he who betrayed us."

The thought shocked Ruth. Selfish? How could he even think that, with James lying in that flag-draped box? She tried to work up indignation, wanted to say something cutting that would defend James. But nothing came except the pain of empty reality.

He was right—James, by his secrecy, had been a coward, even as he led his unit, even as he saved his buddies, even as he died under orders. She looked at Casey, who had only wanted to give James his love, however it was perceived.

"He's gone, and we're still here." Casey's mouth curled into an ironic smile. "We did our duty, too. But I can't do anything for him anymore, and neither can you. He's gone, and we're still alive."

"I made a promise—"

Casey stood and stretched wearily. "I don't think that promise is binding. He doesn't need our protection now, and I don't want to live a lie anymore."

She began to shiver, and Casey reached for her hand and pulled her up.

"Come on," he said. "Let's go back inside. Let's get through today and tomorrow."

Ruth took a deep breath of chilled air and looked once more at the frozen lake, so gray and unwelcoming. But it would melt again, would again sparkle in the sun.

Casey was already walking down the path, and she had to run to catch up.

The Home Team

From my upstairs bedroom window, I can see our back yard where Brendan patiently hurls baseballs toward the old tire suspended by a rope from the big oak, the steady thump of baseball against wooden fence marking a melancholy, almost funereal cadence. It's early March, traditionally the dead of winter in Wisconsin, but the snow is almost gone—global warming, I suppose. Only small gray patches are left in the gullies and shadows, tucked away from the sun like painful memories.

Brendan has already begun thinking about baseball. Not that he ever really *stops* thinking about baseball, though his love for the sport is in direct disproportion to his athletic ability. Even I, his mother, who adores him and lauds everything he does, must admit that he is not very good. His pitches completely miss the tire more often than go through the center. From my angle, he appears much younger than his thirteen years, slender frame vulnerable, hairless chin still smooth as childhood. His throws lack any power or precision, yet he continues, stubborn as the mottled snow-lumps, methodically concentrating on every movement.

I silently curse Denny, as I have every day since he left. I curse him for allowing Brendan to practice baseball alone; I curse him for being so weak that he couldn't stay and work out his problems; I curse him for keeping me hanging, suspended in the air like the tire from the tree, leaving me a life as dingy as the stubborn snow.

And I curse myself for wishing he was still here to reassure Brendan, to help him with his pitching, and to hold me when I cry.

It's been more than two months since I stared in silent shock as Denny jammed his clothes into the big suitcase, stood listening numbly while he coolly explained how things would work.

"You won't have to worry about money, Janie–Al will take care of the store, and I've arranged for you to receive regular checks."

Arranged? When? It sounded as though he had practiced the speech many times. How long had this been brewing? We'd always been happy–at least I'd thought so. We did all the normal stuff–the family vacations, the movie nights, the discussions about medical plans, car insurance, Brendan's grades. If we weren't exactly ecstatic every moment, wasn't that just the way of life? If he wasn't happy, why hadn't he ever said anything? Maybe more important, why hadn't I noticed?

"If you need anything, call," he said, handing me the number of the Colorado ski lodge where he'd arranged a job. Need anything? Like what? Love? Life? Breath? He was taking everything I needed with him.

God knows, once the shock wore off, I wasn't silent–I begged him to tell me what was wrong, why he had to leave, what I could do to change things. But he just shook his head.

"It's nothing you did or didn't do, Janie," he said miserably. "It's me. I just don't fit in my skin, and I've got to get away to think."

Then he began to cry. I'd never seen him cry before, not even when his father died the year before.

"And what about Brendan? What happens to him while you're off finding yourself?" I saw his back stiffen.

"I'll keep in touch with Brendan. It's going to kill me to be away from him. You know how much I love him."

"It's me you don't love," I stated flatly.

He gave me a long, sad look.

And he was gone.

Then came the tears, practically nonstop. I couldn't eat because everything just came right back up, and sleep was a mocking stranger, replaced by late hours of numbly manipulating our game console's sticks and buttons, a mindless distraction that kept me from my empty bed. Oh, I continued with my life, such as it was, moving mechanically about, doing what had to be done. But most of the time I just sat and stared at the game on the TV screen, wishing I could fit the pieces of my life together as neatly as the colorful blocks that fell unceasingly, piling up and disappearing like the empty days.

I finally hit the wall and reconciled with my bed, replacing the empty staring with the sleep I had missed, escaping into oblivion every moment Brendan wasn't around. When he was home, I tried to present some sense of normalcy, but we tiptoed about each other, only our shadows touching.

Denny, to his credit, called every night to talk to Brendan, and after a couple of weeks he began calling me, too, late at night. He'd cry and apologize and try to explain his actions, and I'd cry and beg him to come home. It became a pattern, with even the words the same every night:

Me: "Come home, we'll work it out."

Him: "I can't. I have to figure out what it is I want."

Once I did let my anger out: "What if I decide not to wait until you find yourself?"

Long pause.

When he spoke, his voice was sad. "I guess you have to do what you have to do."

We'd endure long silences, unable to speak, unwilling to hang up. I used up every bit of energy I had wondering what he was doing now, what I'd done wrong, what I would do next. I'd yell, I'd cry, I'd cajole, I'd plead, I'd threaten, and his lack of reaction was the most frightening thing of all. I was drained, wrung out like a sponge. Every time the phone rang, I would jump with both anticipation and anxiety. I dreaded the pain of our conversation but feared more the cessation of the connection.

So now it's March, and still, I cry. And I sleep. And I wait.

My cousin Carla says I'm nuts for holding on.

Three months, kid!" she said this morning. "*You* should file for divorce if he won't. He's had enough time to work things out and come back home. And after all this hell he's put you through, why on earth would you still want him?"

But I do.

I know I shouldn't, but I do.

My family is supportive, but even my mother encourages me to move on. "He's left you, Honey," she says gently. "You've got to face it."

She and Denny's mother, Joan, sit with me and sip tea in awkward silence. Joan is concerned about me, too: she is still my family. Plum Grove is a small town, and our families have always been friends. Before I started dating Denny, I climbed trees in his yard, babysat his little sister, and went caroling with the family. I can see the pain in Joan's eyes, hear the apologies in her voice as she awkwardly talks to me about mundane matters. I know she, too, is confused and hurt by Denny's actions, but she concentrates on Brendan and me, and I silently bless her.

My father says little–verbal communication was never his strong point–but he awkwardly pats my cheek, his eyes vague, hurting for me. "Concentrate on the business at hand, Janie. Sometimes strength is just another word for patience."

None of them fully comprehend that I still love Denny, that I still want him. I tell myself it's not all his fault because I *understand* him, understand the forces that shaped him. I was there when he shattered his pitching arm, losing his baseball scholarship and his chance at the majors. I watched his face when his father berated him, and I held his hand at the man's funeral. I rationalize his pain, his feeling of being trapped, finding solace in commiseration because now it's *my* turn to feel trapped, stuck in a situation not of my making, helpless to change it.

I tell myself that despite all the pain I'm feeling, he's feeling even more. I'm no martyr, but as long as I know—think—he loves me, I can go through anything, wait as long as I have to until he makes up his mind to either come home or cut me loose. Maybe I'm wrong. Maybe I'm crazy. Everything today just seems so—temporary. Something breaks, you throw it out and get a new one. Disappointment is not tolerated, sentiment is passé. What kind of example is that to set for our children?

But as the world turns to spring, my life remains on ice, and I'm cold in my thinning resolve.

Now, with baseball season within sight, Brendan is immersed in his own dream, that of being a major league baseball star, something that will never happen. I know this not only because of what I see, but also because at the end of last year's season, Lew told me so. Lew is Brendan's coach, a big, balding man with a walrus mustache, the guy who took me to my first Homecoming dance a lifetime ago. Divorced and childless, he lives for baseball and "his kids" and has always been wonderful with Brendan.

"He's a great kid, but not pro material," he once said to me. To Brendan, who had just bobbled an easy fly, he called out, "Nice hustle, Buddy! You'll get it next time!"

I wonder if there will be a next time. Brendan moves into the more competitive Senior League this year, and not every Little Leaguer makes the cut.

Baseball was Denny's special connection with Brendon. They spent hours in the park or the yard, throwing and batting, discussing techniques and players. He knew Brendan's limitations but never stopped encouraging him, never made him think he could be anything less than dynamite with a bat and a glove. I could hear them in the backyard, where Denny praised empty swings with shouts of "Nice cut, Champ! Straighten out that arm, and when you connect with the ball, it's gonna travel!" Never *ifs*, always *whens*. But now, everything is an *if*. *IF* Brendan makes the team, *IF* Denny comes home, *IF* the world starts spinning again.

◆

It's one of those false Wisconsin springs where the days are bright and balmy, icy winds a fading memory. Lew has decided to begin his team's practice early because, as he says, "We'll probably have a foot of snow in April." He invites Brendan to come work out with his Little Leaguers, saying it will help refresh his skills before he tries out for Senior League. I go along to each practice and watch Brendan swing into empty air, miss easy flies, trip as he's running.

But I also watch him explaining to the younger kids what they need to do and how they can improve–the same way Denny used to coach him. Brendan cheers the good plays and calls encouragement and advice for the muffed ones. Through four years of Little League, I watched him spend much of the time on the bench, cheering on the better players. Denny would stand behind the fence, applauding small triumphs and calling, "That's all right," to errors, and now I see Brendan offering the same to the younger players. While he himself can't seem to make bat and ball connect, he can explain to the younger kids how their muscles should flex, where their eyes should focus, how their feet, hands, and head should move, how to think like a ballplayer. And when they take his advice, they do better.

Each evening after practice, I hear him on the phone with Denny, going over the day's practice play by play, listening intently to long-distance coaching. When I hear him lower his voice and say, "I miss you, too, Dad," my heart aches, and I don't know if I hurt more for the boy or the man.

I myself have stopped talking to Denny. Two weeks ago, after the last time I did, I thought about our conversation while washing a vase. I rubbed the glass so hard it broke, gashing my hand. As I tried to stanch the blood with a kitchen towel, I decided that enough was enough. Let Brendan keep up his conversations. I was finished talking. So now, each night, I overhear my son say to the phone, "I'll tell her, Dad," and he tells me, but the hope is dry in my throat, and my nod is automatic and empty.

◆

One day I am watching practice when Lew approaches me.

"Why don't you take Brendan out sometimes and let him throw to you? He can use the practice, with his tryouts coming up."

I balk at the idea. "What help would I be? I don't know anything about baseball." I once again silently curse Denny for putting me in this position.

He elbows me with long-honed familiarity. "I seem to recall you were pretty good at softball back in the old days." His familiar smile is comforting. "Just catch for him. Toss the ball and let him practice swinging."

His words stir up my parental guilt. I dig Denny's glove out from the top of the laundry cabinet where it was hidden behind the floor cleaner—as unused lately as the glove. When I slip my hand into the well-worn leather, I can feel the shape of Denny's hand within, almost as though it is once more wrapped around mine, warm and protective. I suddenly can't breathe, and I jerk my hand out and put the glove back up on the shelf.

In the sporting goods section of the hardware store, I pick out a glove for myself. The new-leather smell is pleasant, and Al suggests I work oil into the glove to soften it. He is careful and solicitous in his tone, as are most people lately when they talk to me, as though the wrong words, the wrong tone, will cause me to shatter into a million pieces. It's a tone inherent in a small town, where everyone knows your business, and you have to smile and suck it up and pretend everything's fine so *they* won't feel too bad. Suddenly irritated, I excuse myself in the middle of his discourse and escape.

When Brendan comes home from school, I am sitting on the front steps, working oil into the glove's pocket. I tell him that I need more exercise and thought it would be fun to play ball with him. He looks at me with his summer-sky Denny eyes and thinks a moment, mechanically flipping his blonde hair off his face. I pray he does not see this as confirmation that Denny is never coming home.

"OK," he finally agrees, with an air of superiority, "I guess I could teach you to throw." I am relieved he does not mention Denny as he sits down and examines the new glove, declaring it adequate. I listen as he explains the importance of seasoning a glove, working it until it becomes an extension of the hand rather than a mere covering. His voice takes on the ring of authority as he talks, the most he has spoken to me since Denny left. Maybe the most I have listened.

"The right glove is a perfect fit. It won't be right for anyone else because it's yours alone," he explains, and I recall the feel of Denny's glove on my hand. Brendan keeps talking, and I am impressed by his knowledge of the game. Later, on his orders, I obligingly tuck a ball into the glove's pocket and chuck it under Denny's side of the mattress, thinking maybe it will cause baseball knowledge to seep into my brain while I sleep. Denny likes to spread out when he sleeps, and I got used to pressing my body into a thin line along the edge of my side, sometimes waking with the startled feeling that I am falling off. I wake a lot more lately, keenly aware of the space beside me, and the new lump is strangely comforting.

We begin the next day after school, throwing the ball back and forth. Brendan talks about the rules of the game, explaining the mechanics of pitching, how to let the arm come all the way around, how to gauge when to let go to get maximum speed and a straight trajectory, how to shift your fingers to make the ball move different ways. I dutifully follow his directions, although he is amused at my puny efforts.

"C'mon, Mom, you throw like a girl!" We both laugh. It feels good.

A few days later, Brendan suggests that I run with him. He makes me do sit-ups and stretches before we run, and I feel the aches in muscles long unused. He laughs as I groan and complain, but it's really not a bad feeling. At least there is some feeling there–an assurance that I am alive.

As I feel the figurative dust being jogged from my brain, I notice the actual dust on my computer keys and idly start to surf the Internet. I type in a search for "baseball" and am faced with several million sites, but one marked "Pirate Sam's Blog" catches my eye. As I read the journal of a man who follows the Pittsburgh team, I am struck by the amateurish writing. I see he has a huge following, and ads pop up here and there, providing payment for his efforts. As though carried by awakened blood pumping through my body, ideas start to form in my head, tumbling around, piling up and spilling over; I used to write—the unfinished novel on my computer is testament to an aspiration that got lost in the morass of daily necessities. I need to get back to it. I decide to start with something short and simple, something I can submit to our PTA newsletter. I begin a humorous essay about the parents at Little League games, comparing them to various birds while offering suggestions for positive bleacher protocol.

I find myself suddenly excited by the ideas that pour onto the computer screen, creating words out of thoughts, form out of chaos. My fingers feel light, tapping the keyboard and sliding the mouse, and I am surprised to find that an entire morning slips by where I do not feel tense or agonized, where I do not think about Denny.

The days begin to fall into a pleasant pattern: I do my errands and work at the computer until Brendan comes home, then we exercise together until supper. Afterward, he chatters away and builds the salad while I make supper. Sometimes we find a ball game on TV, and the more Brendan explains as we watch, the more I find myself enjoying the strategies of the game.

I finish the article and take it into the office of the Plum Grove Parks Department, where my friend Denise is in charge of Community Education. She is also president of the PTA and edits the monthly newsletter. She reads the piece and laughs.

"This is perfect. I'll put it in next month. Oh, by the way, Fred Danzinger is retiring this year as the school district's student activities coordinator." She is nonchalant, but her eyes watch me carefully. Your area of expertise."

"My degree's in Communications, not Athletic Scheduling."

"The job could be more than that," she suggests. "I could put a bug in Bernie's ear, and you tell your mom to talk to Cloris." Bernie Caufield is the District Superintendent, and his wife, Cloris, is my mother's bridge partner. Small-town networking. Denise shrugs. "It couldn't hurt to apply. Think about it."

I do think about it. More, I give my mom the go-ahead to push Cloris. I think about how the job could be expanded from merely coordinating athletics to handling all student activities, even writing grants and expanding arts, academics, and athletics programs. My heart beats a little faster as I consider the possibilities, and I exult as though I'd made it to first base on a bunt.

Skimming the local shopper, I notice the ads for Denny's hardware store. They are bleak and boring, done in-house as an afterthought by the bookkeeper. I turn on my graphics program and run up some sample ads for the store. Al likes my work and promises to use them.

The next day I get a call from his wife, Diane, the president of our local theater group. We chat a little about the kids—we were scout leaders together—and she tells me Al has shown her my ads. She was impressed, she says, and asks for my rate to create a brochure for the theater's coming season. I make an appointment with her for the next day to go over some ideas and make a mental note to create a resume and samples to send out to area businesses.

I put in an application for Fred's job. Bernie seems pleased.

Sleep is once more my friend. One morning I find I have moved away from the edge of the mattress, and my body is pressing against the glove lump, so I move it down toward the foot of the bed.

April trickles its drippy way through, and May comes sashaying in. Through the small-town grapevine, I acquire a few local ad accounts—the furniture store, a dress shop, a couple of restaurants—and enjoy spending my days playing with words and graphics. I refresh my knowledge on creating Web sites as well and take out a small ad in the shopper. I look forward to the after-school workouts, to stretching out my legs, and feeling my body work toward exhaustion. I fall asleep with my brain still in gear, devising new writing projects. I begin to feel looser, freer than I have in months. One morning I wake to discover I have moved to the center of the bed and am lying on the sight rise between the depressions from Denny's and my bodies.

Each evening after our final laps, Brendan and I fall exhausted and laughing on the front porch steps. While I sit there gasping for breath and chugging water, he talks about school, about his friends, and about baseball—about everything except Denny. He explains the infield fly rule, details the importance of stealing second, clarifies the definition of a balk. And I am interested because his face, like Denny's—is so animated as he talks.

Once, while explaining to me about batting technique, he forgets himself. "Dad says—" he begins, then stops, looking guiltily at me.

"What does Dad say?" I ask, trying to sound nonchalant, surprised that it's not so hard. He examines my face for signs of cracking and, seeing none, continues cautiously.

"He says that if I can straighten out my swing, I'll really connect." Then he looks down. "But it won't make any difference. I'll still be a lousy player. I just don't have what it takes."

Out of the corner of my eye, I can see him examining my face, looking for something: Encouragement? Honesty? A promise that life will always be fair? I want to smooth his fine hair and tell him it will all be okay. But I know I wouldn't be doing him any favors by making false promises.

"Well, how do you feel about that?" I ask. "I mean, what if you aren't the best player? Can't it still be fun?"

He seems surprised at my answer. "Well, sure, but–'

"Does it change the way you feel about the game? Don't you get the chance to play? Does anyone *else* tell you you're a lousy player? Lew? The other kids?"

Brendan looks puzzled. "No, but–"

"Seems to me the only one who thinks you're a lousy player is you."

He is quiet for a moment. Then he says, "I'm not going to make a team this year."

I digest this information for a moment. My son doesn't need lies at this point.

"You might not," I say, and his eyes go wide at this parental breach. "But the way I see it, you have two choices. You can continue feeling sorry for yourself, or you can work hard, like you've been doing, and give it your best shot!"

"And if I still don't make it?"

"Then you go on from there. If life throws you a curveball, you adjust your swing." He ponders the idea, then nods, and I ruffle up his hair, cornsilk-blonde, and stick-straight, just like Denny's.

I have to keep swinging, too. I have a child to take care of and a shot at a career. I realize I can handle both on my own, and the idea is as exhilarating as stealing second.

◆

Brendan has baseball tryouts today. I perch on the bleachers with the other parents. If Brendan makes the cut, we'll celebrate at Dairy Queen with the other new team members. If he doesn't, we'll drown our sorrows at home with take-out pizza. My father sits next to me, he says to lend moral support, but I'm not sure whether to Brendan or to me. Brendan first gets tested for fielding. He is sent to left field, along with five other boys, and the coach hits flies and grounders to each in turn. Brendan catches or at least stops most of his, and as the boys lope back in, I am surprised to discover I have been holding my breath.

Next, the pitching machine is wheeled in, and the players line up to bat. *Please*, I pray silently as Brendan's turn comes up. His first swing is an overhand chop, coming down miles from the ball. Brendan looks rattled, wriggling his body, shuffling in the dirt, and I feel my nails digging into my thighs.

Suddenly a voice rings out, "C'mon, Champ! Level it off!" Denny's words.

But they've come from my mouth.

Lew turns around from the fence where he and the other coaches are watching. His eyes scan the bleachers, then light on me, and he smiles and nods. Without turning his head, my father reaches over and pats my clenched hand. I feel my cheeks grow hot but keep my eyes on my son, concentrating on the business at hand.

I call out again: "Straighten your arms and let the bat carry you through! Relax!"

Brendan doesn't look around, but I can see his shoulders adjust, see his jaw set as he raises the bat above his shoulder. At the next pitch, he connects, and though it's just a wobbler toward third, he turns to me and grins delightedly. Brendan misses some of the next pitches and hits a few, nothing spectacular. Still, he comes from the plate shooting me a thumbs-up, and I feel that tickle in my nose that usually is followed by tears.

But I am smiling so hard my cheeks hurt.

◆

We're sitting on the back screened porch, where I nurse a beer and Brendan wolfs down pizza with teenage voracity.

"So, you doing okay with not making the team?"

Brendan considers, then nods and swallows. "Yeah, I talked to some of the other guys who didn't make it. We're enough for a couple of teams, and we're going to rotate players and play by ourselves in the park. And I can still help Lew and umpire the little kids' games."

I have to smile at his enthusiasm. "That's a very mature outlook!"

"Yeah, well, I figure when life throws you a curve, you gotta adjust your swing." We share a knowing grin.

The phone rings, and Brendan jumps up to get it. I close the porch door as I hear his “Hi, Dad! Naw, I didn’t make it.” I sip my beer and watch the sun disappear into a glowing amber line. Then Brendan comes out with the phone.

“He wants to talk to you,” he says, his look unsure. A light breeze comes up, but I don't know if that is what causes the little chill that runs up my bare arm. I wait until Brendan grabs another piece of pizza and goes back into the house.

“Hey,” I say into the phone, proud that my voice is so cheery.

“Well, he sounds okay,” Denny’s voice is distant even through the clear connection. “Is he really?”

“I think so.”

There’s the briefest pause. Then: “Are you?”

“I am just fine,” I say, pleased that there’s no sarcasm in my voice.

We exchange a little small talk, discuss some necessary matters, and he asks if I need any money. He doesn’t say if or when he’s coming back, and I don’t ask. After we hang up, I sit looking across the yard. The lemony glow from the sunset is thinning, spreading across the sky, a herald of more cold weather. But spring in Wisconsin is always a tease, and I can be patient, knowing there will be plenty of warm days ahead.

It’s just like baseball. Whatever happens, there’s always another game, another at-bat. You swing, and sometimes you miss, but sometimes you feel that jolt of ball against bat that runs up your arms and jumpstarts your heart, and you run. Sometimes you beat the throw and hit first base, continuing a little beyond, and sometimes you're tagged out, so your trajectory curves back toward the dugout. You never know if you'll make it, but that unknown, that's the thrill of the game. So you make the try, and maybe you'll find yourself rounding third and heading for home.

The Difference

I once read that the human brain gets a new wrinkle for everything we learn. After that, when reading or in school, I'd occasionally try to feel my brain twisting as it filled with knowledge, to feel the subtle crinkling that was certainly going on inside my skull. Growing seemed much the same; after hearing some aunt gush about "what a big boy Sanford is getting to be," I'd strain to feel myself grow, lying still in bed to better discern the stretching of bone and tissue. Of course, as with the brain wrinkles, I never actually *felt* a change, and I turned fourteen believing that growing, like learning, wasn't anything physical that could be described. I learned differently soon enough.

That summer of 1963 began the same as every one before it: as soon as school ended, Dad, Mom, my little sister, Nettie, and I packed up the station wagon and headed for our cottage at Plum Lake, which was located about mid-way between Chicago and Milwaukee, where we lived. There were a lot of lakes in that area, most of them loud with the roar of speedboats and the shouts of transients polluting the beaches. Plum Lake was different in that it had no public easements—families owned the entire shoreline with cottages coexisting with year-round homeowners, all of us scorning the "vacationers" with their loud music and even louder clothing. We were, after all, above them, for we were permanent (albeit on a part-time basis).

Mothers and children were ensconced at the lake while fathers spent hot weekdays in the city, doing whatever work they did to provide the summers of country coolness. There they sweltered in a semi-bachelor existence until Fridays when they joined the line of cars snaking out of the city toward their waiting families.

Meanwhile, the women visited the village beauty shops to create a vision worth traveling to see. The children were scrubbed and dressed up in their casual best and instructed to stay clean while waiting for the exhausted warriors returning from the battlefields astride eight-cylinder steeds. The weekend air was filled with the sweet, pungent smell of barbecue smoke and the deep, alien sound of male laughter.

The rest of the weekend would be spent in a frenzy of such catch-up activities as swimming, horseshoes, and softball. At night we'd fish, pick out constellations, or tell jokes, savoring the closeness that comes with knowing that the end is near, wanting to stretch those warm moments forever. Sunday evenings, our fathers, sunburnt and spent with non-stop "relaxation," returned to the cities to eerily silent homes and skies bright with the artificial glow that washes out the stars.

For those of us left behind, the week maintained a casual open-endedness: housework was reduced to that dictated by basic sanitation; meals were catch-as-you-can; we lived in bathing suits and shorts, with shoes an unnecessary encumbrance,

For those three months of every year, we had an extended family comprised of our summer friends: people I had grown up with, but only during the summer months. The rest of the year, our thoughts revolved around our "real" lives of school and activities, as though the summers were merely a break in life's action, those special friends like company china, packed away to be pulled out when needed.

We relied on one another for companionship, pooling our resources. Each property had its charms: an attic filled with comic books for rainy-day reading, woods for exploring, a flat yard for baseball. The Tuckers on the eastern shore had the best swimming beach, with a gradually sloping, sandy bottom, and it was there that we gathered each day the weather permitted. We divided naturally into groups, each with an unspoken claim to a portion of the beach. The mothers gathered on the grass beyond the sand, beneath the sharp drop of a large bluff where, in the cooling shade of birches and elms, they could gossip and play bridge or mah-jongg, keeping watchful eyes on their children. Nearby, sandy-bottomed babies-built sand mountains and valleys while toddlers and young children played in the wet sand at the water's edge or splashed noisily within the shallow confines of the pier.

My group was the oldest, nearly a dozen in number. Up until that time, we had always been equals, but this year was different. Somehow, the girls had magically become young women over the winter, with musical giggles and budding bosoms. Perched on the raft, they preened and posed, stretching bronzed legs and tossing their hair to catch the sunlight as I, watching, caught my breath. Most of the boys had passed through the agonies of puberty relatively unscathed, emerging as slightly acned Adonises, flexing new muscles, and comparing beard growth, real or anticipated. My androgynous cronies of summers past had somehow, terrifyingly, divided into *boys* and *girls*.

And I belonged to neither group.

I was, to be blunt, grossly misshapen: grotesquely tall and skinny, with useless balloons for hands and feet that dangled clumsily from overlong arms and legs. These defects, safely hidden beneath bulky winter clothing, were all too apparent in shorts and T-shirts or–heaven forbid–a swimsuit. Worst of all, a shiny metal grill filled my mouth, a beacon illuminating my deformities. None of the other guys were so freakish. Even their voices had mostly settled into a comfortable pitch, while mine still floated through several octaves at whim, a sound not unlike the static created by quickly spinning the radio dial. Their bodies were Cadillacs, seeming to be all original parts; mine was a rebuilt Chevy.

Of course, they all acted as if my loathsomeness didn't matter, but I knew they were just being kind, so I retreated into the guise of the reclusive intellectual. Above childish games, I stretched out on the sand with the thickest book I could find at the town library, nonchalantly ignoring their calls to join in.

"C'mon, Sandy!" they'd yell. "We need you on our side!" But I'd stretch a closed-mouthed smile and wave my book as though it were too good to put down. Even Judy Applebaum couldn't entice me into an inner-tube war; still, it was agony to endure their fun! I don't remember one word of *Quentin Durward*, but I'll never forget Judy's squeals as she was tossed off the raft.

My parents worried a little about my self-imposed solitude, but I insisted everything was fine, and they finally left me alone, assuming it was merely some normal teenage insanity. My sister Nettie, my only confidant, was more blunt.

"Sandy Marcus, you are a jerk! You're blowing a whole summer over some dumb Ichabod Crane complex! C'mon, all those guys are just as freaky!" How could she understand what I was going through? At ten, she was quick and bright and bursting with self-confidence. She would never be sickeningly adolescent, afraid, and unsure. I was alone. Everyone fit in someplace, except me.

And Rose.

Rose Feinstein was a tall, bland child-woman–back then, we referred to people like her as "simple." Her coloring was pallid, hair like corn silk, pale eyes vapid as distilled water. In fact, all her features appeared slightly blurred, as though seen through water. She was somewhere in her late thirties, but her age was hard to tell, belied by an aura of childlike innocence. She seldom spoke, never initiated a conversation. We had known Rose all our lives–she was like a cousin we knew we should be nice to. Though we always asked her to join games, she'd just smile shyly and shake her head. Sometimes she would venture into the water in her baggy, long-skirted swimsuit. There, she'd just stand, waist-deep, contentedly splashing as children paddled tolerantly around her.

Rose's mother, Elaine, a war widow, was a retired teacher who had made Rose the focus of her life, hovering around her daughter, wrapping her in a faded yellow chenille robe when Rose came out of the water, watching out of the corner of one eye even while playing cards. She was sure Rose could never function without her, so she made sure she never had to.

Most mornings, Elaine would make Rose sit on a blanket in the shade and, with a small audience of children in attendance, would comb her daughter's pale, waist-length hair. First, she would unwind the tightly coiled braids and gently loosen the plaiting. After carefully combing out any snarls in the fine, fair hair, Elaine would brush it until it gleamed, the blondness phosphorescent in the shadows. Then Elaine would carefully reform the braids and coil them once more about Rose's head, all the while talking soothingly, telling Rose how she'd always take care of her. Throughout the monologue, Rose would sit perfectly still, her eyes fixed on the lake and the raucous action that was invariably taking place on and around the raft.

And so the summer passed, as did every summer, in a blur of bright light and soft breezes, and, for me this year, in the agony of self-imposed loneliness. The last Sunday night before Labor Day, everyone traditionally joined together at a bonfire on the beach to recap the summer and discuss winter plans. The next day we cottage dwellers would be packing up our summers, closing up the cottages, and making the short, jarring trip back to the world of schedules and planning.

We huddled around the fire, roasting wieners and marshmallows on stretched-out coat hangers, telling jokes, and singing songs. After a while, my group broke away from the fire and traipsed to the water's edge to skip stones and talk teenage talk. I held back, but Ben Wasserman grabbed my arm and pulled me along. This year, rejoining the world held a certain magic for the eight oldest kids, for we would be entering high school. We were spread out over two different cities and had always attended different schools, but this year, some of us would be going to the same high schools, together in the "real world" for the first time. Everyone else lived in Chicago, and no one would be attending my school, so their excitement didn't concern me. I said nothing, methodically skipping stones on the calm, dark water as they chattered on, making plans to meet the first day and compare notes.

Judy had been uncharacteristically silent throughout the banter, and finally, she burst out, "It's not fair! Dad just told me today that he's been transferred, and we're moving to Milwaukee. I'll be going to some dumb old Marshall High School, and I don't know anyone there at all!"

I couldn't believe it! Marshall was my school! Of course, she didn't know that, but when I tried to say something, I found my words tangled up behind my braces. The others consoled Judy on her bad luck, and before I could say anything, her mother came over and said it was time to leave, and she was gone.

That night I couldn't sleep. It was one of those almost-autumn nights when the air, still warm with summer memories, is tinged with a smoky crispness, the unmistakable harbinger of fall. The moon was rising full and golden as I crept from my cot, pulled on a pair of shorts, and slunk from the cottage. I ran barefoot, following along the upper path on the east side of the lake until I reached the bluff overlooking the beach. There, I flung myself down on the soft bank, my breath coming in swells, my mind fielding wildly bouncing thoughts about lost chances, about Judy, and about my silent stupidity.

I lay there mentally bemoaning my grossness when I heard someone coming down the lower path along the shore. I peered into the darkness and felt a slightly eerie, electric shock down my back. There, running along the path, was Rose, wrapped in her robe. The soft paleness of her hair and robe glowed eerily in the shadows. She was puffing and stumbled once in the undergrowth but regained her balance and continued running, her inhuman gasping wild, like that of a frightened, desperate animal. Something kept me silent, and I crouched lower in the grass, watching. She must have run all the way from her cabin, and when she stopped on the beach, she was panting, hunched over, clutching the robe about her. As her breathing gradually slowed, she straightened up and stared at the water, seemingly mesmerized by the night satin. Never taking her eyes from the lake, she reached up and tugged at her braids. As they fell, she ran her fingers through to pull them apart, shaking her head to release a river of moonlit silver. She emitted a wild, high laugh that gave me the shivers and flung the robe from her body to the sand, grinding her heel into it. I gasped.

She was completely naked.

Her body, always hidden by sagging, shapeless clothes, was slender. Her skin gleamed ivory in the bright moonlight as she stood leaning, her body curving toward the water as though drawn toward some magnetic force. The pull irresistible, Rose stepped into the water, her movements tentative and graceful as a deer. She splashed her toes and squealed softly, delighting in the silky, warm wetness. An owl screeched, and she recoiled for a moment, her head tipped, listening. The bird hooted again, and the sound echoed across the water. Rose relaxed and stretched out her arms as though reaching for the sound.

Then she walked slowly into the lake. The water covered her knees, then her hips, while her arms trailed behind her, and her hair floated, iridescent, unreal, on the rising water, the train of a fairy queen. When she neared the end of the pier where the lake bottom dropped sharply, she didn't stop, and I frantically thought, *Holy Jeez, she's gonna drown herself!* I started to panic, wondering what to do.

Then she started to swim.

She used no recognizable stroke, but Rose was obviously working to move in the water. Slowly, she moved out toward the raft, her labored breathing audible above the gentle splashing. I held my breath, and after what seemed an eternity, she reached the raft, grabbed the ladder, and awkwardly pulled herself and sat, doubled over, breathing hard. After a while, she stretched out on her stomach, then turned over to lie a time on her back, then flipped over onto her stomach again. It hit me that she was "sunbathing" on the raft, imitating the girls.

After a while of that, she sat up and moved to the edge, dangling her feet in the water. I watched, fascinated, as she kicked and splashed, giggling and posing, apparently teasing and flirting with invisible admirers, a surreal imitation of the girls we had both watched all summer.

I don't know how long this went on, but when Rose reluctantly moved to the ladder and lowered herself back into the water, the moon was far in its descent, casting a shimmering path across the water. She repeated her strange, awkward stroke until she reached the shallows, then walked heavily through the water to the beach, where, dripping over the discarded robe, her body drooped back to the familiar, resigned posture. Picking up the robe, she half-heartedly shook the sand out of it and wrapped it about her now-shivering body. After one long, mournful look at the lake, she turned and disappeared slowly back into the brush.

My eyes were wet as I watched her go. All that longing, that yearning to be like the others–how well I understood it. I turned over and lay staring up at the stars, feeling a dull pain in my heart that throbbed as though wanting to leap from my body. I knew–I guess I had always known–that I would outgrow my differences. Mine were just temporary discrepancies. Poor Rose would never be what she wanted to be. We were joined in our disparities yet separated by our certainties. It didn't seem fair, somehow, and I pondered the newness of the injustice for a long time before I finally got up and headed back to the cottage.

The next day was hectic with packing, but for the first time that summer, I really wanted to go swimming. Taking a break, I ran to the beach. Judy was there, crouched at the edge of the water, idly drawing her fingers through the soft, wet sand. Throwing caution to the winds, I ran over and crouched next to her.

"Where are you moving to?" I asked.

She pouted prettily. "Dad said it was on a Vienna Street, near Sixty-Second Street somewhere."

"Hey, I just live a few blocks away, on Melvina!"

She looked delighted. "Really? That's wonderful!"

She said it was wonderful! I gulped and plunged on. "I'm going to Marshall, too." There. It was said. I stood up and braced for the worst. Let her cut me down with a cold, "That's nice, Sandy, see you around." I was prepared to die.

"Oh, I'm so glad!" she smiled broadly up at me. "I was so scared—you know, with moving and all, and not knowing anyone. It'll help so much to have such a good friend there!" She reached up and, dazzled by that smile, I took her hand and pulled her to her feet. She laughed at the clinging wet sand she had transferred to my hand from hers and brushed it away gently, still holding my hand as she continued, "My folks have your phone number. Can I call you when we move? Could you maybe show me around?"

"Sure." How casual and cool! I was her good friend! She was happy we'd be in school together! She was holding my hand! Now I could die, and happily.

"I wish I could be more like you," she was saying, and I stared at her. "I mean, you're so mature, reading all those books and not acting silly like the other boys." My burst of laughter must have surprised her, but she joined in. I was trying to think of something mature to say when her mother called her to help pack, and she ran off, leaving me with a handful of warm sand and a promise to call as soon as she moved.

I stood very still for a moment, sniffing the fading scent of her suntan oil. Then, with a whoop, I flew off the end of the pier in a decidedly immature cannonball.

◆

Settling into the routine of school, I learned a lot about Judy—and about myself—and what I learned surprised me. I'd always seen her as being the perfect cheerleader—cute and perky. I had envisioned us at basketball games—me the star player, her the head cheerleader. Instead, I discovered that she was actually very shy and didn't enjoy being the center of attention. She joined the photography club and took pictures for the school newspaper.

It was just as well because I also discovered that my basic clumsiness was not the fault of puberty but simply a fact of my life. Leaving my hoop dreams behind, I also joined the paper as a writer. All those summer novels had helped my English skills enormously, and my teacher suggested that I had some real writing talent. It became part of the persona all high-school students acquire—you're The Jock, or The Brain, or The Artist. I became The Writer. Judy was The Photographer.

We remained friends, hanging out together sometimes but dating others as well. In the "real world" there seemed to be so many more choices than in our private little lake society. Still, sometimes a random comment or event would bring up a memory of a past summer, and we would smile or laugh together at the private joke. We knew the lake summers would always be a bond, keeping our shared memories warm as a welcoming fire in a cold world.

That summer was to be my last long stretch at Plum Lake. Toward the end of the school year, I persuaded my dad to find me a job on the newspaper where he was an editor. I was just a gofer, but I paid attention and learned a lot—enough to know that writing had to be my future. But having a job meant the end of my carefree, lazy summers. Mom and Nettie still spent the weeks there while I entered the other side of summer, joining my dad in the ranks of the weekend commuters. Judy was still there, as was most of the old gang, and we spent weekends trying to recapture the fun we'd had as children, playing games on the raft, lying in the night grass, and telling stories, but things were different. Our numbers would dwindle in the coming years as we drifted away to summer jobs or different kinds of vacations—car trips, theme parks, backpacking. Times were changing. We were changing.

But Rose was still there. Nothing had changed for her, and I knew nothing ever would. She still sat at the beach, shimmering in the shade, splashing with the kids, wearing the same baggy suit, the same vague smile. I wondered if she still stole moments in the moonlight, but I never tried to catch her at it. I had been an intruder that night and felt I owed her the respect of privacy. God knows, she had little else of her own.

I did spend many hours by the water, dreaming my own dreams. As the ripples softly hit the pier, I could hear in those little splats the solitary squeals and giggles of a moonlit night. Sometimes I would pick wildflowers and drop them into the water to watch them disappear as the current gently carried them to the far shore. I was different myself, no longer a child, not yet a man. I could see beyond today, and the future was vast and exciting. But behind my closed eyes was burned the image that would never change, that would haunt me all my life: Rose standing on the edge of the water, yearning, reaching for echoes, her body curving to meet the moonlight.

Home Again

Alan Cramer entered his last semester at the University of Wisconsin with the confidence of a successful used-car salesman, secure in a future assured by his certain, imminent acceptance into the university's law school

Law school had long been his dream, more than a means to an end, nearly an end in itself. He felt he had properly prepared for that dream since high school, where he excelled in Mock Trial and Debate. In college, he majored in History—a decision applauded by his undergraduate academic advisor, a small woman with large teeth and the comforting habit of offering him jellybeans. His LSAT scores had been acceptable, if not spectacular, his grades good in general courses and excellent in his major. Hounding the law school office, he finally learned that he was "on the list."

Feeling he'd covered all the bases, Alan settled into a final term packed with blow-off courses, which he proceeded to treat accordingly, his advisor's assurance that the last semester "didn't really count" ringing in his ears. He ignored job fairs and corporate interviews, certain he was set, above the panic of others not so sure. He was sure that all of his activities were unnecessary, mere inserts in his life's true trajectory, nothing more than parentheticals.

So it was with great shock, after graduating with a slightly lower grade point than he'd had going into that final semester, that he discovered that he had not been welcomed into the ranks of law students. He might have blamed the economy for an overabundance of law school applicants. He might have blamed his roommate for encouraging him to "party hearty." He might have blamed Janel for dumping him and wrecking his concentration. And he might have blamed his advisor for not telling him that, yes, the application committee would definitely consider his final semester grades. In the end, he reluctantly blamed himself for being shortsighted and arrogant, so sure he would be accepted that he hadn't even applied anywhere else.

On graduation day, he found himself seated with his thousands of classmates in the cavernous Kohl Center, half-listening to some political figure he didn't recognize extolling the virtues of his education and the certainty of his future contribution to society. He was lost in his own mental self-flagellation when the guy next to him pulled a six-pack from under his robe.

"Cheer up, man. Life's just beginning!"

Alan replied glumly, "Got cut from law school."

"Bummer. Here." Alan accepted the offered beer. Hell, his parents wouldn't be able to see him in that sea of black crepe. Ironically funereal, he thought, looking at the cheerful masking tape message *Hi Mom* on the mortarboard of the girl in front of him.

"Here's to the future, man!" the guy held up his beer in salute.

"Or the lack thereof," Alan said as they tinked cans and drank.

"You got a place to go?" The guy took another gulp.

"Home, I guess."

"Warm bed, loving parents, free food?"

"Something like that."

"Could be worse."

Alan wasn't sure he agreed. As their row stood to cross the stage and receive their diplomas, the guy set his can down and, with his foot, pushed it under the seat in front of him. It tipped over and drops of remaining beer puddled around it. Alan drained his own can and set it upright under his seat, mentally promising to chuck both cans in the trash on the way out. He'd made enough messes.

He arrived home less a conquering hero than a whipped puppy, only slightly more embarrassed than his parents, who nevertheless dutifully threw him a graduation party at which he assured friends and relatives that he had "many irons in the fire." Indeed, he had none.

The one saving grace was seeing Christine again. He realized how much he'd missed her when, with a grin of her small, slightly skewed teeth, she handed him a little stuffed bear in a graduation cap and gown with a tag that read, *When the real world gets un-BEAR-able, remember you've always got a friend.*

"God, Chrissie, you're the best. Why did we ever break up?"

She curled an unruly lock of dark hair around her ear, a habit he found endearingly familiar. "It was a mutual decision, remember? We were going off to different colleges, meeting new people. We had big plans."

Alan looked at her. "Yeah. Right. Plans. So, what happened?"

She shrugged. "Man plans, God laughs."

Alan knew exactly how familiar Christine was with plans going awry. Her mother had developed cancer during the spring of Christine's sophomore year at Eau Claire, and she stayed home the following year, against her parents' wishes. After her mother died, Christine took a job at the local candy factory and stayed on to help out with her younger brothers, Nate and Kenny.

"You should have gone back to school like your dad wanted," Alan said.

"How could I leave him and the boys?" she shrugged, then added softly, "You know, though, I would never have gotten through that time without you."

"I didn't do anything."

"You were there. All the times you had me come visit you! You got me dates, made me get out and have fun. You have no idea how much that meant to me." They were by a table loaded with sweets, and she untwisted a sandwich cookie and gave half to him, a ritual established back in third grade.

"So, you screwed up. What now?" she asked, licking the cream from her half of the cookie. Of course, Christine would voice the thought no one else dared speak.

He shrugged. "They got any openings at the candy factory?"

"What, you want to get fat like me?" She patted her hips which, like the rest of her, were ample but not unpleasing.

"I'm serious. I need a job. They hiring?"

She shook her head, her hair a dark storm swirling around her tiny face. "It's slow. They're even laying off. You'll find something. Hey, you got a college degree! That's gotta open some doors!"

"Oh, yeah, my history degree. I already got an offer to be the head curator of the Field Museum. They're begging for my sheepshead expertise!" Alan laughed ruefully.

"C'mon. Something will turn up."

He glanced at his mother, chatting with his Aunt Carol. She beamed at him as though everything was fine, and he felt a deep twang of guilt at her unyielding devotion. Somehow, the fact that his parents didn't express any disappointment hurt him more than if they had whined about his errors. He turned back to Christine.

"I really screwed up this time."

"God, Al, why the hell didn't you apply anywhere else?" She picked up a lemon bar.

"I just figured my acceptance was a given. And UW's the best. You know, I just wanted to get someplace."

"Well, you got someplace all right," she said as she stuffed a bit of the lemon bar into Alan's mouth. The tart taste was sour. "Back home, just like me."

◆

He went back to the summer job he'd held since high school, a lifeguard at the city pool. There he sat in the rosy shade cast by the red beach umbrella. Evenings he hung out with Christine, often seeking inappropriate places to have quick sex. They rolled in the grass under the high school bleachers or sought the closed, darkened beach, where they bumped awkwardly inside the confines of the crisscrossed lifeguard tower, once almost getting caught in the sweep of police lights, holding their breath and later laughing at the adventure.

At night Alan lay in the narrow bed of his youth, staring at the dark shapes of high school awards and memorabilia that decorated his room. The vapor light over the garage reflected wanly off his two diplomas, high school and college, which his mother had hung in identical frames on the wall behind the door.

At first, his mother cheerfully fell into the old routine, washing and folding his laundry, picking up his room, cleaning his bathroom. But in July, she rebelled.

"Alan, enough is enough. You know how to work the washing machine, and I am not your servant." He was in the family room playing the ancient Nintendo of his youth, and she indicated the pile of dishes he had accumulated on the coffee table. "And your room stinks. If you want to live like that, please keep the door closed, so the smell doesn't pollute the rest of the house.

Shame washed over him. "Oh. Okay, Ma." He picked up the dishes and carried them into the kitchen. His mother eyed him as he rinsed the dishes and put them in the dishwasher.

"Honey," she said, not unkindly, "you can't spend your life on the couch playing video games."

His response was to buy a hand-held video player, where he shut the door and spent off-duty hours in half-darkness, mindlessly killing off ghosts and racking up points.

As the summer progressed, his parents began dropping not-so-subtle suggestions about looking for real work for the fall.

"Martin's always has openings," his father suggested, referring to the town's hardware store. "If you like, I could call Hink."

Alan cringed at the thought. "I don't need my daddy finding me a job," he snapped and immediately felt bad about his retort. "Sorry, Dad. Thanks, but I'll find something on my own."

So, in August, he bought a suit at Kohl's, trimmed his shaggy hair, and began applying for jobs in Milwaukee and Racine, the closest cities to Plum Grove. He had assembled an impressive, only slightly exaggerated resume and actually got called for a few interviews. The first three were ambitious attempts to start at the top, but the results were jolts of reality.

"Son, this is a professional position. We're really looking for someone with a master's degree and five years of experience."

He polished his confident response: "Sir, I can learn anything faster and do it better than anyone!"

One interviewer looked amused at his argument and said, not unkindly, "I appreciate your confidence. Come back when you have some experience in the field."

He was persistent. "Well, I do have a college degree, sir. That should show that I have abilities."

"But we need some tangible proof of real-world success, as in job experience."

The next five interviews were for unexciting, lower-tier jobs, but the responses were just as negative and just as frustrating:

"Sorry, son, but I'm afraid you're overqualified."

"How can I be overqualified if I haven't done anything?"

He bemoaned the Catch-22 to Christine. "I'm either underqualified or overqualified," he complained. "No middle ground." They were at her house, painting the shutters she had lined up against the inside garage wall. Nate and Kenny were washing the car in the driveway, getting more water on themselves than on the car. Their shrieks of laughter floated into the high, clear September sky. "I'm going to be stuck in this town forever. With or without a job."

"I'm not," Christine declared, scraping her brush on the side of the paint can. "The candy factory is for now. Maybe that's what you have to concentrate on, Al. Right now. Set your sights a little lower. Just until you have a plan."

So he let his father call Hink Martin and grudgingly took a job at the hardware store, where he wore a green vest and a plastic pin with "Alan" printed in cheerful blue letters, and where the customers were people he had known his whole life.

"So, Alan, it must be nice for your parents to have you home. Exactly thirty-two inches, dear." Mrs. Geary watched him warily as he measured window screening for her.

"Yes, Ma'am," he said, making the mark for the cut.

"Is that thirty-two inches? Exact? I'm not paying for more." She hadn't changed since he'd delivered her paper when he was a kid.

"It's okay, Mrs. Geary. Mr. Martin says to always give a little bit more, just to be sure. No extra charge."

"You know, Alan," she said, watching him intently as he cut, "lots of our young people come back here after college," she said. "It's no shame. It's a good place to live."

"Yes, Ma'am," he said, running the slicing blade along the screen just a little harder than necessary. "I'm just here taking some time off after school."

"Of course, Dear," she said without conviction.

He rolled and tied the screen, marked the slip, and handed both to her, not quite meeting her eyes.

"Thank you, Alan," she said and patted his cheek, just as she had done when he collected for the paper. "You're a good boy." She left, his cheek burning from her solicitous touch.

◆

He felt better about living at home by paying a small rent and began to help out more, taking some small pleasure out of mowing the lawn, picking up around the house, and even vacuuming. He began buying some groceries and one day surprised his parents by making dinner for them—a stew that his mother called a "valiant first effort."

A few of his old buddies had taken jobs and stayed in town, and occasionally he went out with them to a movie or to a bar or concert in the city, but most of his time was spent with Christine, old habits being comfortable as a well-worn coat. As autumn rolled on, they hung out at Lou's Grill, where they had spent so many Fridays after high school games. Now they worked their way through the crowded dining room to get to the bar, passing by the tables and booths where they had hung out as kids. He was struck by how young everyone there was, the kids in their letter jackets or black on black clothing, the piercings and tats, the weird hairstyles. They were so young, so hopeful. Alan found it depressing.

"D'jever think we'd be in the bar?" he commented to Christine one night as they wove through the young crowd and settled on stools at the end of the bar.

"God, remember how we envied those guys in there? They were, like, the cream of the town."

"Yeah, remember how Whitey Johnson was always at the back booth, telling the story about the time he caught that long pass to win the game against Sauk River."

"Ssssh," Christine hissed. He followed her eyes to the far end of the bar. There sat the legend himself, older and a little pudgier around the neck and middle. He was telling a story, and from his gesticulations, it was obvious he was again reliving his big catch. Alan turned away, snickering, and caught a glimpse of himself in the mirror behind the bar. He had an unnerving flash of himself on the same stools in five years, ten, fifteen.

His beer suddenly tasted bitter.

Other times, he and Christine retraced the shadows of their past footsteps to the park, the schoolyard, or to nearby towns where they pretended they were carefree tourists just visiting. In January, they cleared a patch on the lake and skated, giving it up to some kids who showed up wanting to play hockey. It had always been easy with Christine, and they spent hours talking, finding comfort in their mutual stagnation. Sometimes he compared Christine with Janel—moody, exciting, unpredictable Janel. She had been a bubblehead, but they'd laughed a lot. Funny, but now he couldn't remember a single conversation. He appreciated the steadiness Christine had that Janel, for all her sexiness, had lacked.

He found himself wondering if Christine was comparing him to anyone.

◆

With March came the soft air redolent with a teasing promise of spring. One Friday night, Alan and Christine decided to go roller skating. Neither had been to the rink in years and as they sat lacing on their rented skates, Alan watched the shouting, hooting skaters circling beneath the revolving mirror ball. Nothing had changed. The terrible acoustics blended the blaring music together with the rough hum of skates on wood and the shouts of a children's birthday party going on in the table area. The smell of pizza, popcorn, and warm bodies blended into a comfortable mulligan, and for a moment, Alan was back in junior high, zipping about, skating backward, showing off in the center of the circle.

He looked around, and it occurred to him that, aside from a few parents holding the hands of their small children, he and Christine were the oldest people there. A young couple, maybe 12 or 13, rolled in front of them. The girl wore a short black lace dress above shiny black leggings. The boy's hair, bleached the color of oat straw, was spiked in numerous points above his head, his baggy, low-hanging pants in danger of being tangled up in his skate wheels. The two held hands as they skated awkwardly around in the circle.

"Look at them," Christine nudged him, speaking above the music. "Were we ever that young?"

Alan suddenly couldn't breathe. He watched the couple hit the far curve and begin their return. "I gotta get out of here."

Christine was already unlacing her skates.

In the dark parking lot, they tumbled without a word into the back seat and thrust desperately together, unzipping, clutching, rocking, pushing hard against the other as though to exorcise the ghosts they'd seen in the rink.

◆

He called her the next morning. "Do you or your brothers have plans for the weekend?"

"Not that I know of."

"Let's go camping," he said.

"Are you nuts? It's still winter."

"We'll just go one night. The ground's thawed. It's supposed to hit thc 50's today. Come on. The boys'll love it. And don't you need to get away?"

She was quiet a moment. "We can be ready in an hour."

They decided on McKlusky State Park, a wildlife preserve about 10 miles out of town. There was a large campground with bathroom facilities and hiking trails. Alan dug around in the attic and found a tent, sleeping bags, and camping utensils and packed some cans in a backpack. His car was too little to handle people and equipment, so he borrowed his dad's pickup with "Cramer Plumbing" emblazoned across the side.

Christine and her brothers were sitting on their porch steps, all three clad in layers of flannel and corduroy. As Alan got out, Kenny, the younger brother, came running up to throw sleeping bags in the truck bed. "Hey, Al, Thanks! This'll be great!"

"Anytime, Punk." He affectionately ruffled Kenny's bushy dark curls, shocked that the boy, at 13, was nearly as tall as himself, while fifteen-year-old Nate was eye to eye, a fact he found surrealistically disturbing.

"My God, Chrissy, what happened to the two munchkins who used to ride on my back?"

Christine laughed at his chagrined look. "They grew up, Al. It happens."

They set up two tents near the creek at the park, far enough from the bathrooms to feel remote yet near enough to be accessible when needed. The earth was damp with thaw, but Christine had brought oilcloths to spread on the ground while Alan unloaded the firewood filched from his parent's garage. They finished setting up and ate the sandwiches Christine had brought.

"C'mon, let's go for a hike." Alan brushed the crumbs off his pants and headed for a far copse of trees with Christine close behind, leaping lightly over tall tufts of dry, colorless grass while Nate and Kenny whooped and ran ahead, jumping and tumbling.

They worked their way through the thicket of shrubs and brush that presaged the trees, weaving around the thick undergrowth and broad trunks while snapping phone photos of each other, of rock formations, of anything that moved. They entered a deep stand of evergreens where slanted sunlight feathered softly through the thick needles. The air there was refrigerated by stubborn smudges of snow, and they could see their breath as they jostled each other through the small clearings in an intermittent game of tag.

Alan and Christine broke through together into a section where the trees, instead of growing haphazardly, were in obvious rows, the open areas less bushy, scored with wood-mulched paths. There was an odd familiarity to the place, and Alan searched his mind as they walked, finally lodging on a memory.

"Hey, Chrissie, don't you know where we are? This is the school forest!"

She looked around. "For real?"

The park had a partnership with the school district for school science class field trips where students planted trees and analyzed the creek water. Now the little group stood among a topiary dynasty, each successive line of trees one year newer than the next.

"Remember when we all came out here and planted our trees for Arbor Day?" Christine gazed around. "God, Al, I haven't been here since seventh grade!"

"Yeah, my class planted our trees somewhere over there," Nate said, indicating a vague direction. "We could see the highway from our section."

"We plant this year," Kenny said, looking around.

Suddenly, Kenny gave Christine a shove, shouted, "You're it!" and dodged away through the trees.

They all ran, chasing and swinging around the tree trunks, laughing and shouting, and finally collapsing against a large, whorled rock.

Christine gasped to catch her breath and looked around. "Hey, do you remember where our class section is?" They wandered around, checking the various small signs that indicated the school and year the trees were planted.

"Over here!" Alan yelled, and Christine joined him. He was standing by a small, neat sign that read, *Lakeview School 8th Grade, 2010*. They stared at the straight, tall grove behind the sign.

"Look at that," Christine said, her voice low and awed. "Nine years."

Alan could only nod, recalling the slender young trees with diminutive leaves they had planted. He remembered the bus trip from school that day to this place where the saplings had already been unloaded and sat waiting for them. Under Ms. Ulmstad's direction, the students had dug deep holes and then carefully lowered the burlap-wrapped root balls down. They cut away the covering and spread the roots, covering them with soft earth they patted down around the saplings. Then, filling buckets from the tank on the ranger's truck, the students reverently poured the water to soak the soft earth around each tree. Alan recalled with a flash of clarity the vastness of the sky that day, wide and open above them. Now, that sky was barely visible, webbed with branches from those same trees. The ground was dark and sodden, the leaves from last fall mulching down in their cyclical return to the earth.

"You know, Mrs. DuBois called and asked if I would come help out with Mock Trial this year," he said. "She said I had always been the best high school lawyer she'd had." His short laugh was a bitter snort. Christine didn't say anything. "Come on," he turned. "Let's go back."

They stepped out of the forest to a sun low in a cold lemon sky. Nate and Kenny searched the area for deer trails while Alan and Christine stood still in the washed saffron light, surrounded by the moldering smell of decomposition and the encroaching chill of the evening.

"We'd better head back to camp," Christine murmured, as though reluctant to break the spell.

They loped along in the waning light, through evergreen and brush to the grassy fields beyond. The sound of trickling water led them to the creek, which they followed back to camp. Alan artfully arranged the wood over kindling and soon had a blaze going. He set a cooking grate over the fire and put a heavy cast iron frying pan on top. Into a pat of sizzling butter, he spread corned beef hash from a tin, cracking eggs on the top.

"I'm impressed," Christine said, sniffing the sizzling food.

"I'm going for my cooking badge."

They both laughed.

Kenny, who had been across from them, poking the fire with a stick, suddenly looked up at the sky behind them.

"Cool. Look."

They turned. Where the sun had set, a fiery selvage blazed, then diffused upward, blanching to paler pink to yellow to pale blue, blending into the darker sky above. Almost imperceptibly, tiny stars that weren't there a moment ago twinkled faintly, growing bolder and joined by others in the deepening dusk. Above the eastern horizon, a glow developed in unimpressive competition with the sunset, casting the reminder of civilization just a few miles down the road. The little group ate in comfortable silence, listening to the breeze whisper through the tall dead grass.

Alan put a pot of water on to boil for instant cocoa, and Christine produced a package of oatmeal sandwich cookies for dessert.

"I didn't have time to get stuff for s'mores," she apologized.

"S'okay," Alan said, pleased that Kenny laughed at the joke. "These are great."

Nate and Kenny spread their sleeping bags in their tent and crawled in to escape the night chill. Alan and Christine sidled together and threw a blanket around their shoulders. Faces aglow in the lambent flames, they laughed and told stories until a gentle snoring revealed that the boys had fallen asleep.

They sat watching the stars in companionable silence, enjoying the night breeze cool on their blanketed backs, the fire warm on their faces. The musty smell of earth mingled pleasantly with the fresh, slightly fishy scent from the creek. Somewhere in the distance, a coyote sent up a cry, echoed eerily by others, and in the clear, still air, it was impossible to tell if they were near or far away. Alan tipped Christine's face to his, and they kissed, tentatively at first, like new lovers, then crept into the second tent, giggling and whispering so as not to wake the boys as they rolled together beneath a blanket. Afterward, enfolded in each other's arms, they lay in the partial glow of the campfire just beyond the tent opening.

Christine finally broke the silence. "I'm going back to school in the fall," she said. Her cheek was nestled into the hollow of Alan's clavicle, her breath warm against his skin. "Dad and I discussed it, and he thinks it's time. I'm going into pre-med." she shifted and sat up looking at him, her eyes reflecting the dying fire outside the opening. "What about you?"

He pulled the blanket up against the now-chilly space that wanted her warmth. "I'd make a lousy doctor."

Christine laughed.

He considered her announcement. "How'd you decide this? You never talked about medicine before."

"My mom. I watched her go through all those tests and trials. The doctors never gave up on her. They made her feel hopeful, even when there was no hope. I want to give hope, and I want to make hopes reality. God, I sound like a drug commercial." She turned away to reach for a snack bag, and Alan saw her make a quick swipe at her eyes.

She tossed him a plastic-wrapped cookie. "So, what about you? What are you going to do?"

"I don't know," he said, tearing the wrapper with his teeth. "Do you believe that there's really some grand plan? Like we're destined to eat dirt first in order to find our real direction?"

"Do I believe in fate? Nah, we make our own fate."

"You think so? Look, you were going to be a teacher. If you hadn't quit school to take care of your mom, you'd probably be doing that now instead of thinking about being a doctor. It really wasn't your decision. You see what I mean?"

Christine considered the idea. "Yeah, okay, but it was my decision to come home, though I'll grant you the result was maybe unplanned. What about you? What dirt did you eat?"

"Well," he lay back down and pulled the blanket up to his chin. "You know, at first, I blamed everyone but me." He took another bite of the cookie, thinking as he chewed. "But it was my decision to be stupid, to just roll over and die."

She pulled another cookie from its wrapper, twisted it, and handed him half. At that simple movement, Alan felt a sudden flood of a familiarity laced with warmth.

She licked the frosting from her cookie. "So, what should you have done?"

He stared at her, enjoying the picture of her little kitten tongue lapping the cookie. "I should have kept trying." His head suddenly felt clear. "Hell, I still can. I can retake the LSAT." The words seemed to come by themselves. "I'll only have lost a couple of years." He was starting to feel excited as he spoke the words that made it seem real.

He took a deep, cleansing breath of the sharp air, then pulled her down to his chest and kissed her, a long, lingering kiss different from those of the past year—not just entertainment. You could go home again. It just wouldn't be the same.

It could be better.

She snuggled closer, and he tucked the blanket around her. "Starting over is good," she said.

They lay without speaking, warm within the blanket, and gazed through the tent flap at the darkened sky, where a thin crescent moon hung like a closing parenthesis.

The First

I wasn't in the best mood to visit that day as it was, and I certainly wasn't looking forward to having someone who had once danced at a presidential ball ask me to pull down her diaper-pants so she could use the toilet. I had fought with Brad that morning, and my future was as hazy as my grandmother's past. After three years together, Brad wanted marriage, a mortgage, a joint health savings account. He wanted forever, and I wanted—I didn't know what.

"Jesus, Mel," he had said that morning as he unloaded the dishwasher. "Why are you so afraid of commitment!"

"What's the use?" I argued. "In the end, we all leave anyhow one way or another. And maybe death is the kinder way out."

"You are so morbid." He slammed the dishwasher door, and I stormed out alone to face my grandmother, the proof of my point.

Brad usually came with me on my visits, and because he hadn't known my grandmother before her dementia, he served as a buffer between me and the Gram I knew less and less each visit. He was able to accept this imperfect copy, this out-of-focus imitation of my Gram. The worst of it was that I resented what she had become—this stranger who had stolen my real Gram's body and who only let me see the occasional glimpse of her, playing some macabre baby game of peek-a-boo, with her the baby.

I went over every Saturday morning to give my grandfather a little respite, a chance to run some errands or play a round of golf. At 72, he was still tall and strong, with a smile that showed large, original teeth. He could outlast me on the tennis court or golf course, although lately his partner for both had been Gerta, a woman he had met at the senior center. The rest of my family accepted their "dates," but I was ambivalent, a little uncomfortable with the arrangement. I sometimes wondered what their relationship really was but forced myself to admit it was none of my business. Besides, he was devoted to Gram and deserved a little fun. God knows his life with Gram these past few years had been anything but fun.

A niggling voice in the back of my head kept wondering if either future was in store for me.

Grampa was wearing his natty golf clothes and looked delighted to see me. "Thanks so much for coming today, Mellie. I could use some exercise, and it's such a beautiful day." He looked out the door. "Where's Brad?"

"Just me today," I said, not elaborating. No sense in giving him something else to worry about. "How's she doing?"

His smile wavered a moment. "Pretty good," he said. "We had a little trouble this morning—she didn't want me, a 'strange man,' helping her get dressed." He gave a sad little chuckle, and I hugged him before we went into the living room.

Gram was sitting on the sofa, impeccably dressed as usual in the flowered blouse and pink slacks that Grampa had selected for her.

"Melanie's here, Lizzie." He sat down next to her, and I squatted in front.

"Hi, Gram!" I tried to sound cheerful, but she just stared at me, then turned to Grampa.

"I'm cold," she said.

"Here you go, Sweetheart." Grampa pulled a quilt off the back of the couch and tucked it around her knees. The pieced fabric, handmade by her own grandmother in once-bright scraps of color and pattern, was faded from use and sunlight.

"I'm going out for a bit, Lizzie," Grampa said as he combed her hair with his fingers, fluffing it like cotton around her heart-shaped face. Physically, she looked like the Gram I remembered, and for a moment, I could almost believe that a miracle had happened, that she was fine. Almost believe. I knew there were no miracles. I knew that sometimes God simply gave up on you and left you on your own, twisting in the wind.

She looked at him, her eyes recriminating. "You're leaving me."

"Just for a little while." Seeing his pain, I had a fleeting, selfish wish that he would decide to stay, which would set me free. With a rush of guilt, I shook off the feeling.

"Go," I said, pushing him toward the door. "Don't worry. We'll be fine." I had a sudden flash of my grandmother saying the exact same thing to my parents as she pushed them out the door when I was little, and she was babysitting me. Ironic. "Have a great game. Go, Gerta's waiting."

Watching him set his green cabbie cap at a jaunty angle and hoist his golf bag over his shoulder, I guiltily prayed I'd inherited his genes instead of Gram's. Then I took a deep breath and went back to the living room, hoping for the best.

"Who are you?" My grandmother peered at me through milk-chocolate eyes.

"It's me, Gram, Melanie. I'm here to keep you company while Grampa runs some errands." While he escapes for just a little while, I thought, wondering how he could survive living with a woman who only occasionally even remembered who he was.

"Melanie." She tasted the name, apparently sifting through the Swiss cheese of her mind for the hole that held a memory. "The architect. Theresa's girl."

I relaxed a bit. Maybe we'd have a good day. "That's right, Gram."

"Theresa's my sister. I have two sons," she said, and my ease disappeared.

"No, Gram, no sons. Only one daughter. Theresa. My mother."

"I don't have two sons?"

"No, Gram. Just Theresa." I brightened. "But Theresa has two sons! My brothers, Tom and Jason." I grasped at the thought that maybe that's where she got the idea. I was always looking for connections, for reasons for her comments, to assure me that her mind wasn't gone, just jumbled.

"Theresa. She has red hair."

"That's right. Well, she used to anyway. It's blonde this month."

"If she doesn't stop with the dye, it's going to all fall out someday. But then I suppose she could buy some wigs in different colors."

I laughed, and she laughed back. That was the old Gram, tart as a green apple. Then her eyes went blank, and she was gone again, giving me a sharp, familiar jolt. I wondered where her mind was taking her now and wished I could get inside and see what she saw. Maybe she was off in another time or even another world of who knows what imagination sparked by malfunctioning synapses. I hoped that at least she was happy there. It was hard on my grandfather, but he wanted to keep her home as long as possible, and he cared for her with the patience of a new lover coupled with the devotion of a lifetime.

The familiar room was decorated with photographs of people who floated through her mind's half-light. She had always been a meticulous organizer, creating elaborate scrapbooks long before the hobby became popular, preserving beloved faces that were now strange to her. Looking around at the careful documentations, I couldn't help feeling angry at how she—and Gramps—had been cheated, promises be damned! And Brad wanted me to commit for a lifetime?

I fell into my visit routine, scanning the framed photos and sifting through the albums neatly stacked on the étagère for a picture that might spark her memory. I selected two photographs and settled into the brocade chair across from where she sat wrapped in the quilt. The coffee table between us held neat stacks of magazines and a small silver tray, upon which was a bottle of water, a clean glass, and two different seven-day pill containers—a white one for morning medication and a blue one for evening. Each week Grampa counted out pills and filled the little chambers so as to administer the correct medications—a tangible reminder of a segmented life.

My grandmother reclined on a buffet of pillows. Two were faced with handmade stitching, one of which proclaimed "Love," and another "Home," each in an ornate embroidered heart. The industrious hands that had made those hopeful proclamations were now restless and unguided, now clutching the faded quilt, now shredding tissues into bits.

"Tell me about this picture, Gram," I began the morning's entertainment by holding the first photograph up before her eyes. It was one of my favorites, a childhood photo of her and my great-uncle Thomas, astride a large horse. The animal's sides gleamed in shades of photo-gray, and the curly-headed tot in front clutched its mane in her chubby fingers while the older boy sat behind, his arms wrapped around her.

"I don't know," she said, setting her mouth into a pout.

"Gram, that's you," I prodded. "Who's that with you?"

She peered closer, adjusting her glasses, staring, trying to make sense of the images. Unsuccessful, she sank back against the pillows.

"I don't know," she said, handing it back. There was a sadness in her eyes, but then she brightened. "I had a horse once," she said. "We called it Topsy. My brother Tom and I rode it. Bareback."

"Yes," I said, excited by the connection, however slight. "This is you and Tom on Topsy, Gram."

She looked at the photo again. She was silent a moment. Then her eyes cleared. "Tom died in Korea. He was a First

Lieutenant. He sent me a Kimono, red with purple dragons embroidered all over it. We got the telegram before the package came. When I put it on, it was like Tom was hugging me." Her fingers skimmed Tom's face in the photo. "Do you have any brothers?"

Peek-a-boo.

"Yes, Gram. Two. Tom and Jason. Tom's named for your brother."

"Tom?" Her lip trembled, and I hurried to the next photograph, hoping it would be a happy memory.

"Here, what about this one?" I asked, holding up an old photo of a smiling girl in a fluffy party dress. I loved that photo of her, labeled Elizabeth, Prom, 1954. The background colors had paled to a faint steel blue, and the yellow of the dress and the red of the girl's lipstick stood out as bright splashes of color. She stared straight into the camera with the confidence of youth, the knowing gaze sending a mixture of innocence and sex through the Kodachrome wash. My grandmother peered through her glasses at the photo, then leaned on her pillows.

"That's me," she said. "I was seventeen."

Good for you, Gram, I thought, feeling as elated as if I had won the Pritzker Prize.

She continued. "It was a dance. There was a boy…What was his name?" I had used the photo before, but she had never mentioned a boy, and I wanted to keep her talking, to mine this new information.

"What dance? What boy? Gram, you been holding out on us?" I joked, hoping to keep her mind working by unearthing some gentle girlish memory. She ran gnarled fingers over the photo.

"I was seventeen," she repeated. The girl in the photo held a demure pose, but the dress revealed the budding woman, its sweetheart neckline dipping above a soft swell of breasts while the cinched waist and fluffy skirt emphasized the kind of womanly curves that never go out of vogue. I watched my grandmother's lips move as though seeking appropriate words and waited for her memory to kick in.

I tried prodding her. "You were quite the babe, Gram."

She snapped to. "A babe, huh? You bet I was." I grinned.

"And the boy?"

"What boy?"

"You said there was a boy. Was this before Grampa?"

She thought a moment. "A boy. Yes. The boy. He took me to that dance. He wore a blue suit. Eyes the color of the ocean, you could swim in them. Handsomest boy I'd ever seen. I would ever see. What was his name?" She ran her fingers across her dry, cross-patterned lips. "He was my first."

I felt a slight current run through me. Her first? Her first what? I wasn't sure I wanted to know, yet curiosity got the better of me. Besides, she was on a roll, and I wanted to keep her talking.

"Your first boyfriend, Gram?"

"Yes, my first boyfriend," she said, a coquette peeking out from behind the cataracts. "And also my first—you know. My first."

I tried to take in what she was implying. One never thinks of one's grandmother in terms of having sex, and it wasn't a thought I wanted rolling around loose in my mind. But her moments of lucidity were decreasing, and I needed to know what had happened, needed the reassurance that her life wasn't just reduced to a random series of disjointed events that, in the end, meant nothing.

"He brought me a wrist corsage of white roses and baby's breath. The card read *Roses for Remembrance*. The band was a little loose, so I had to wear it higher up, and the flowers bounced against my elbow." She rubbed her elbow as though pushing something up her arm. "Every girl at the dance copied me." Her eyes were soft. "And him in that beautiful blue suit. I pulled one of the rosebuds off the corsage and tucked it into his buttonhole. White against that blue. When we danced, the petals brushed my cheek like gentle little lips. I can still smell them, still feel them."

She closed her eyes, sliding her fingers again across her mouth. I knew that her sense of smell had long ago deserted her, but somewhere in her ravaged brain must have remained the scent of roses, tucked away to be taken out and savored long after the actuality has faded.

I wondered what memories would stay with me to the end. In a flash, I could see Brad. His socks scrunched down around his toes, his heels bare as he pads around the house; the cleft in his chin twitching as he laughs; his off-key serenades while I lounge in the bathtub; his thumb gently gliding down the side of my nose just before he kisses me.

Gram was still talking, and I suddenly felt like a voyeur. I had no right to these memories; they were hers. But I was mesmerized by the rapt look on her face and couldn't speak as she went on.

"Afterwards, we walked to the park. There was a little stream running through—the rush of the water over the stones. We sat on the bank under a big oak tree where the leaves made a big shadow, a big blue moon shadow. Everything was blue, the air, his suit, his eyes..." Her voice lowered to a whisper as she focused on the screen behind her eyelids upon which her movie played. She was no longer an old woman on a couch telling her granddaughter a tale of long ago. Now was then: she was young, sitting in the moonlight beside the stream.

"The smell of the water and the rustle of my skirts pushed up around my waist..." I wanted to cut in but didn't, instead watching her hands as they flickered about her body. "His lips, his arms, his hands, the cool grass higher and higher on the back of my legs." Her voice faded, and she sighed deeply, her body sagging, exhausted from the effort. My fingers touched my cheek and came away wet.

"How I loved him," her voice was tiny, as though coming from the outside in. "That beautiful boy, my true love in the blue suit, in my mind, in my arms, always him." A tear escaped her closed eyes and trailed down to fill a crease at the corner of her mouth. "Oh, what was his name? What was his name?"

She looked at me, her eyes suddenly afraid. "I missed my curfew and told my parents we had car trouble. Don't tell my father," she said, her voice hushed, secretive. My heart wrenched, and I couldn't speak. "Please. He'll kill me if he finds out."

I just nodded, and she smiled and sank back, closing her eyes again. She seemed to be dozing for a few minutes, then she opened her eyes and looked at me as though first realizing I was there. "Who are you?"

My voice trembled. "It's me, Gram, Melanie. Theresa's daughter."

"Melanie." She tasted the name on her tongue. "Who's Theresa?"

She fell asleep then, and I eased her legs up on the couch and covered her fully with the quilt. I spent the rest of the visit staring, first at her and then at the photograph. I wondered if my grandfather knew. I wondered if I would ever forget Brad's name, or if he would remain just a nameless bright spot in my decaying memory.

And then I wondered if she had made the whole thing up, if it was some fantasy. After all, there was no boy in the picture. That thought made me sadder than I had been since she had first begun slipping away. Perhaps she had indeed been unhappy in her life, missing something—a boy with eyes the color of the ocean. How can we ever know what dwells in another's heart?

"Hello, I'm back!" My grandfather's cheerful voice was a welcome relief. I sprang from my chair, and Gram awoke as he entered the room. "How's my girl?" He bent and kissed Gram's forehead, then asked, "Did you and Mellie have a nice visit?"

"You weren't here," Gram scolded.

He smoothed her hair. "I'm back now," he said, his voice tender. "I'll get you some juice."

We went to the kitchen, where he poured three glasses of juice. "So, which photos did you two talk about today?"

"The one with her and Tom on the horse and the one of her in a yellow dress," I said, reluctant to go into any detail. But he just nodded, satisfied, taking a drink.

"Her senior prom. One of my favorites," he said. "She was a real knockout, your grandmother." I followed him into the living room, where he handed Gram the juice.

"Drink it all," he said. "It's orange juice. Your favorite." She looked at him for assurance, and he nodded, so she drank. I thought of how Brad brought me soup when I was sick and sat with me to make sure I finished it all.

He took her empty glass and kissed her forehead. We went back into the kitchen. "I still have the rose she stuck in my lapel that night. You know, when I look at her now, I still see the girl in the yellow dress."

I looked, really looked at his eyes. The irises, even faded by years and sun, were the color of the ocean. Relief washed over me, then sadness at the thought that she didn't even know it had been him. He started to wash the glasses, rubbing each harder than seemed necessary. "I've arranged for a home health aide to start next week. Just a couple of hours each morning."

"Grampa," I hesitated, afraid I was venturing into dangerous waters. But I had to know. "What if—if you had known back then?"

His back was to me, and I saw it stiffen a little. "Known what?"

"You know, about how Gram—things—would turn out?"

“Would I still have married her?” He turned back to me. “I don’t know, Mellie. I can’t answer something like that. I like to think it wouldn’t have made a difference, but how can we ever know something like that?” He shrugged. “Do I wish things were different? Sure, of course.” He patted my cheek. “But not everything.”

I hugged him at the door. “I’ll stop by Wednesday night,” I said. “I’ll pick up some takeout, and we’ll all have supper together.”

He nodded. “That sounds good. She likes Chinese. Usually.”

“I’ll bring Brad, too.”

“Good.” He winked at me. “He’s a keeper.”

“He is.”

I called Brad from the car. “I’m heading back.”

“How was she today?”

“About the same, good and bad. I missed you.”

“I hate it when we fight,” he said.

“Me, too. And we will fight, and we’ll have bad times. But we’ll have good times to remember, too, and I think I can handle it all. At least I want to try.” There was silence on the other end, and I held my breath, waiting. Finally, I spoke. “Are you there?”

“I’ll always be here. Come home.”

Retreat

Catherine Macomber swore at the ubiquitous Wisconsin highway construction that had turned her pleasant commute to Milwaukee into Dante's Fifth Circle of Hell. The irritation was compounded this morning by the blatantly phallic Hummer that swaggered over the line on her left, crowding her lane and forcing her little Corolla to slow down so the leviathan could lumber in ahead. The construction was just one small part of the swelling weal of aggravation her life had become since her husband's sudden departure six months ago, but it was compounded by today's traffic and her old Corolla's annoying habit of arbitrarily locking and unlocking its doors with loud clicks as she drove.

The road narrowed to one lane up ahead, and Catherine slammed on the gas and pulled around the Hummer, whose fat-faced driver gazed down at her with superior disdain. As she passed, she found a perverse pleasure in sticking her hand through the open sun roof, middle finger raised, chuckling at what she imagined must be his shocked look at being flipped off by a fiftyish matron in jeans. It was a small moment of triumph, but one that faded with the memory that today she and the other members of Traverse Publishing were venturing into the country to experience "team-building in a rustic setting." Just what she needed—another example of how she was too old, too fat, too used-up to be part of Romy Vaccaro's younger, fresher, more energetic regime.

But she had to go along, had to keep her job—especially now. Michael's request for a divorce had been a complete shock, and her life became a disjointed dream punctuated by regular, annoying voicemail messages from him, updating her on the progress of their divorce and urging her to call him:

C'mon, Catherine, we have to talk about things. We need to put the house on the market. I'll be fair—we'll split the money.

Catherine, you're being childish. We have to get moving on this thing.

At least have your lawyer call mine.

She would play each message over several times, but never returned his calls.

"You gotta talk to him sometime, Mom," her son, Eli, said one Saturday. He had come over to install the new printer she had purchased after Michael took theirs—his—to his new apartment.

"No, I don't," she responded. "I didn't ask for the divorce, and I'll be damned if I'll make it easier on him. Besides, she couldn't bear the thought of selling the house. She loved the big, open space echoing with years of children's voices, loved the colors she'd painted, the touches she'd bestowed, loved even the familiar shadows that lurked in the corners and floated across the walls at night.

At least she had the solace of her job at Traverse, establishing editorial order out of authors' literary chaos. When the position of Managing Editor came open she applied, feeling she had earned it through fourteen years of dedication. But the job was given to the new, youthful face of Romy

Vaccaro. Suddenly a kid, a baby, barely older than her son, was her new boss.

Summoning all her courage, she had marched into the publisher's office, plate of homemade cookies in hand, and asked point-blank why she hadn't gotten the job. Larry seemed genuinely surprised as he took a cookie.

"Mmmm. Butter pecan, my favorite," he said, munching. "Catherine, it's a managerial position. You're a great editor, and I need you at the project level. Besides, with the divorce and all, you've been a little—overwhelmed. The timing was off."

"Oh," she said and turned to go, but was angry enough to turn back. "At least how about a raise?"

Larry smiled. "Good for you!" He shook his head. "But still off on the timing."

At home, the silent questions about Michael pulsed like living things. Sometimes she sat staring at nothing, wondering where it had all gone, and if, in fact, any of it had been real.

Sometimes she would vent, writing horrible, hateful things in her journal, curses first against Michael and then against Romy, venom that spewed forth as icy comfort. Then she would tear out the pages and shred them, unnerved by her own unexpected virulence.

God forbid anyone should read her thoughts and know the horrible person she really was.

Now she pulled into the office lot and parked across from the small bus Romy had rented to take them to the country lodge, site of her certain humiliation. Pulling out her overnight bag, she plastered a smile on her face and waved at Shanthi, the Creative Director.

She would just have to get through the next three days.

◆

The lodge was rustic-appearing yet obviously upscale, set on the edge of a small lake that serenely mirrored the lush autumnal woods cuddled around its perimeter. Romy had banned all electronic devices, including cell phones, but the Edenlike promise of clean, quiet air was no comfort to Catherine. She saw it only as another chance for her to prove her insignificance, this time on a more primal, physical level.

They headed inside the lodge to register and gazed appreciatively at the comfortable surroundings. The expansive lobby featured leather chairs and sofas grouped around an enormous central fireplace. Muted flute music played from speakers hidden in lush green plantings, and hand-carved signs indicated a ballroom and two meeting rooms down one carpeted hallway and a pool, spa, and fitness center down a second passage. A sign advertised *The Hart and Hound*, a restaurant with a menu posted advertising the day's specials as venison *en croûte* and fresh lake trout with garlic-stuffed morels.

"This is a retreat?" Jim, a copyeditor, looked around at the posh surroundings. "I could get used to this!"

"Don't worry," said the woman behind the desk. "You'll be roughing it all right." She made a call, and within minutes a bearded young man in a plaid flannel shirt came bounding in from the back.

"I'm Seth," he said, shaking hands all around. "I'll be your facilitator. Sort of a corporate activities director. "You guys get the cabins, so say goodbye to civilization, grab your bags and let's get started!"

He led them down a manicured lawn to a dense woods with a dirt path that they followed to a clearing decorated with gigantic tree-trunk carvings of woodland animals. A dozen log cabins with numbered doors were grouped around, and Romy handed out a roommate assignment sheet.

"Find your bunks and stow your gear," Seth said. "Then meet at the fire pit down that path."

Shanthi scanned the list. "C'mon, Catherine, we're in cabin 3 with Carol and Lisa." Inside the cabin, two sets of bunk beds hugged the side walls. "You want upper or lower?" Shanthi asked.

"Doesn't matter," Catherine shrugged but was grateful when Shanthi threw her duffel bag on an upper bunk. There was no ladder, and Catherine had no desire to look ridiculous trying to scramble her ample butt onto the top bunk. Carol opened the back door to reveal a small, basic bathroom. "Well, at least there's indoor plumbing. Water pipes mean there has to be heat, too."

She laughed. "Life is good."

Catherine wasn't so sure.

A whistle sounded outside, and Lisa laughed. "C'mon, let's go play."

They joined the others at the fire pit, where Seth began by explaining the rules. "While the retreat is designed to be fun, there's a purpose to the games. They're for trust and team-building, designed to get you all to know each other better so you can work together more effectively."

Catherine's brain burned. *Huh, most of us have worked together for years,* she thought. *The only real outsider is Romy.* Teamwork. What was more of a team effort than marriage? Yet that, too, had proved untrustworthy. And she was supposed to trust Romy—trust anyone— now?

"We'll start with something simple," Seth said and instructed them to make a tight, shoulder-to-shoulder circle. "This is a trust circle. One person stands in the center and just falls backward, stiff. You have to trust that the others will catch you." Catherine felt a shiver of terror in her chest. She'd fallen a lot lately, and no one had caught her yet.

"Who'll volunteer to start?" Seth looked around. Everyone avoided his eyes. Carol giggled and shook her head.

"Well, I guess it's up to me to be a leader," Romy said. He stepped into the circle, closed his eyes, stiffened, and let himself fall like a pillar of lead. Jim caught him with a grunt, and they passed the stiffened body around the circle. Catherine resisted the desire to drop him when he came to her, instead pushing him quickly onto Gary at her left. They passed Romy completely around the circle, and he straightened up to cheers. One by one, each person took a turn, and though there were some false starts and a lot of laughter, no one hit the ground. Catherine demurred until she was the last one left.

"C'mon, Cath," Romy said. "We each have to have a turn."

He was grinning. She hated that diminution of her name—it always made her think of a urine catheter. She resisted the urge to slap the smirk off his face and stepped to the center, clamped her eyes shut, and tensed, determined to try. But each time she started to fall back, one foot darted back to catch her, and she found it impossible to allow herself to drop.

"C'mon, Cath," she heard Romy's voice call. "We'll catch you. Squeeze in, everyone, no holes to fall through." She could feel the circle tighten in around her, but that very closeness smothered her, and she felt a constriction in her chest. Please, God, don't let me have a heart attack now! She begged silently. Romy would probably be the one to give her CPR, and then she'd owe him her life.

"I can't," she hung her head and stepped back into the wall of the group. "Sorry. I've got a sinus infection, and it hurts to lean." The excuse sounded ridiculous even to her, but Romy was sympathetic.

"Hey, I hear you. Those things are murder." She thought he sounded patronizing as he patted her shoulder. "Okay, Seth, what's next?" Relief flooded her, followed by annoyance. She didn't need the little bastard's affirmation.

Seth divided the group into two teams and passed out blue vests to one team and yellow to the other, then led them to where several ropes were stretched between two trees, creating a wall of randomly-spaced strips with one team on each side. The object of the game was to get the entire team on the other side of the ropes. The trick came when Seth explained that only one person at a time could be passed over or through by the rest of the team. Once on the other side, team members could not help. The goal was to get the team members to work together as the passing side dwindled and it became more complicated to lift and move a person through. A coin toss designated which group went first.

Catherine knew she couldn't keep using excuses, and she hoped no one would call her on the sinus thing when it was her turn this time. She would just have to grit her teeth and do her best.

For the next two days, they participated in similar games during which Catherine noticed that Romy never volunteered ideas until others had the chance to speak, but then they always seemed to use his plans anyway. Each noon they stopped for lunch set up by camp personnel, followed by more games. At four, the participants were allowed off on their own to enjoy the grounds, hiking through the woods or kayaking on the lake until supper, which they ate around the fire pit while discussing the day's activities. Catherine noticed Romy was always the center of the group, his laughter louder than anyone's, his perfect smile flashing in the firelight. The bunks weren't the most comfortable, and she had developed a constant headache, her neck feeling like a rubber band that had been twisted to the point of knotting, each peal of Romy's laughter warping in another knot.

By the third and final day, Catherine began to relax a little, enough to start to enjoy the activities. When they had to try a zip line, she balked for a moment, then closed her eyes and, clutching her pulley line, jumped from the starting platform. To her surprise, she felt no fear, only exhilaration as she sliced through the air. It was the freest she'd felt in months, and she didn't even mind Romy's condescending tone as he patted her back and said, "See, Cath, you did it!"

The final activity was a paintball game of "Capture the Flag." They were each given beige coveralls, which Seth said would help protect their bodies from the force of the paintballs, explaining, "They're harmless, but they do sting." As they pulled the bulky outfits on, Seth drew names to divide the group into two teams. Catherine groaned inwardly when she and Romy were put on the same team.

"You're yellow then," Seth said to them, digging in the gear bag and tossing yellow gloves and vests to each member, then doing likewise for the blue team. "Gear up, and don't forget your eye protection." They received guns preloaded with paintballs in the team colors. Catherine cringed as Seth handed her a real-looking rifle, painted an incongruous hot pink. She hated guns, had refused to allow them to her children even as toys, but even as the weapon in her hands repulsed her, she also recognized a sudden, confusing thrill from within at its heft.

They were standing in the middle of the paintball course, a haphazard collection of color-spattered barrels, straw bales, and large wooden spools that littered the field. At either end waved a large flag—one yellow, one blue—and in the center was an enormous tire mountain with a PVC pipe sticking up about four feet above the pile. Seth blew his whistle once for attention while Catherine struggled to fit her bifocals comfortably beneath the protective goggles.

"Okay, this is the course. You've got fifteen minutes to capture the other team's flag and anchor it in the center pipe. The first team to do so wins. Rule Number One: If you get shot by a paintball, throw up your hands, shout 'I'm shot,' and walk off the field." He grinned. "This includes friendly fire, folks, so know where you're aiming and watch out for a slip of the finger. These babies have hair triggers." He had everyone take a practice shot at the wall on one side to prove it. Catherine was surprised at how easily the shot burst and at the odd gratification she felt at the resulting splat.

Seth indicated high, protective walls at either side. "Take your position and get ready to move out on my whistle." Each team scrambled for its designated bunker.

"Okay, team, let's work together and protect each other's backs!" Romy yelled as they hunkered down behind their protective wall, waiting for the whistle. Catherine sighed and readjusted her eyewear, trying to relieve the pressure on her nose.

The whistle blew, and Romy leaped over the top, screaming, "Let's go, Yellow!"

They dodged through, trying to avoid the blue "bullets" that plopped and spattered around them. Romy charged with a roar, rolling behind barrels, shooting, spinning, moving down the field. Catherine ran to the nearest shield, a large cable spool turned on its side, and crouched down behind it as Carol, running behind her, was splattered with blue. "I'm shot!" Carol yelled, then raised her arms and walked off the field. Catherine considered how easy it would be just to stand up and be shot so this humiliation would be over, but she stayed hunkered down behind the spool.

As members of both sides dwindled, the pellet fire became more intermittent. Catherine peeked out during a lull. Romy had worked his way to the other side of the field and retrieved the blue flag. Now he waved it as he charged back to the center. From her hiding place, she watched as he reached the center and climbed the tires toward the pipe in triumph, waving the bit of blue and shouting, "Victory!"

She felt a bitter taste rise in her mouth. He had won. *He* had won! *Him!* She watched Romy ascend the pile of tires, shouting his triumph. Then, just as Romy reached the pipe before he could place the flag, he was hit on the back with a paintball.

A yellow one.

Catherine looked down at her gun, at her finger on the trigger. She hadn't done it consciously, but there it was. She had shot him. He was "dead." Romy, reacting to the blow according to the rules, set down the flag and raised his hands.

"I'm shot!" he shouted, then looked down and saw her standing there. "Cath, it's up to you. Get the flag!" He worked his way down the pile and started to walk off the field when another shot hit him. "Hey! I'm already dead!" He shouted. He looked around at his "injury" and, seeing the yellow splotch, turned to Catherine, his face not angry, just quizzical.

She shot again.

And again. And again, holding the automatic trigger down, so paint pellets repeatedly peppered Romy's body.

"Hey!" he yelled. "What the hell—?" he backed up, reacting to each hit, and she had a momentary vision of the last scene in *Bonnie and Clyde*, where the bodies were repeatedly shot, jerking in slow motion. He backed away, but she kept after him, taking a perverse pleasure in every hard little splat that would surely leave a bruise on his smooth young skin. She realized she was grinning even as hot tears steamed up her glasses and goggles.

Everyone else had stopped running and was standing, watching. The flag lay a barely-noticed blue blur in her peripheral vision as she kept her eye on the yellow target before her, fuzzy through her double layers of eyewear, foggy from her tears.

"Cathy! Stop! Cath! Hey!" Romy yelled, and every diminution of her name increased her satisfaction with each pop-pop-pop of the gun.

She kept pumping pellets, sobbing, and shooting the man on the ground with arms thrown up to protect his head, trying to roll away from her. Finally, her gun clicked empty. Exhausted, she collapsed in tears and sank to the ground next to the curled yellow form. No one moved. The air was still except for Catherine's gasping sobs and the soft swish of wind through trees.

Finally realizing the pummeling had ended, Romy stirred, sat up, and pulled off his paint-covered goggles to stare at the shuddering figure next to him. The group gathered around them, silent, shocked by the mayhem they had witnessed. Then Romy stood and looked around at the stunned group.

"Okay, that's all, folks," he called. "Game's over." No one moved. Romy stared a moment at the weeping mess next to him, then straightened up. "It's okay, gang! She's quite the actress, isn't she? Really got into it. Nice job, Cath!" She stopped sobbing and stared at him as he did a quick jog around the circled group, fist-bumping each member of the two teams.

"That's right. This was all planned. Just wanted to show you what NOT to do, how it can destroy a team when you don't work together!" Someone giggled, and then they were all laughing. "Okay, we'll call it a tie, right? Great job, everybody! Hand in your gear, then go back to the lodge and get some dinner. The bus leaves at seven. We'll meet Monday first thing to discuss everything." He looked at Catherine, still sniffling on the ground. "Everything."

He stretched out a hand to her, and, confused, Catherine took it and struggled to her feet, dazed and hiccupping. As the group started to move down the path, she handed her gun and goggles to Seth and, zombie-like, turned to follow the others. Romy fell in alongside her.

"Man, Lady, you need anger management therapy!" He spoke in a low voice, and she was grateful for his discretion. "That was not a normal reaction."

"I'm—really, I'm so sorry. I don't know what came over me," she lied. She knew, and she would have done it again, even if the gun had been real, and that was what frightened her to her core. Where had that violence come from?

She looked at him, standing there covered in yellow paint, and realized with a shock that he was not the enemy. Yet she had just tried to kill him; she'd really wanted to kill him.

"I mean it," he said. "You need some help."

"I know," she said.

He nodded. "On the practical side, your health insurance should cover it."

Relief washed over her. "So, I'm not fired?"

"And lose the heart and soul of the business? Not to mention the cookies?" His face went serious. "I know you've had a rough time of it lately." She must have looked surprised because he shrugged. "It's a small office. There are no secrets."

"Thank you," she said. "You're a good boss."

To her surprise, she meant it.

◆

Traffic was light on the way home, the soft late-summer twilight infused with a gray-pink glow from the fading sunset. Catherine anticipated a long tub soak to ease the muscle twinges caused by three days of unaccustomed activity. Her head swam with thoughts of the day, the three days, the hundreds and thousands of days past. She had to look ahead to the days to come and move forward. Monday, she would talk to HR and find a good therapist.

As she drove, the car doors randomly locked and unlocked, and she decided it was time to get a new car. It was time for a lot of new things, and suddenly she looked forward to experiencing them. Change could be good if she embraced it. But memories could be good, too, gentle and persistent as the shadows on the walls.

When she got home, she would call Michael and tell him she wanted to keep the house, and they'd talk it out.

The Night My Mother Danced With Fred MacMurray

I was at our Northbrook restaurant overseeing an upcoming wedding reception when I got the call from my wife.

"We're taking your mother to the hospital—Northwestern, downtown." Caitlyn lowered her voice. "You'd better come now." I gripped the phone and didn't speak. "Jack? Should I send Joni to get you?"

"I can drive."

When I got to the hospital, Caitlyn and our granddaughter Joni were in the ER cubicle where my mother lay still amidst the soft swish of machines.

"Lily, he's here," Caitlyn whispered and stepped aside for me.

At 93, my mother's skin was still velvety and translucent, and even the deep furrows created by life's slaps and punches seemed softened. Faint blue shadows crisscrossed her skin, and the vein at her temple fluttered. Small flesh-colored suction cups peeked out above her loose gown, their wires running to a machine that translated her life beat into a jagged electronic line. Colorless liquid dripped through a tube to the IV needle taped down on the back of her hand. I held her other hand while Caitlyn leaned her head on my shoulder to complete the circuit.

"It was a massive attack," the doctor said. I hadn't even noticed him standing there. "I don't know how she's hung on this long."

"She was waiting for her boy," Caitlyn said. Helpless, I adjusted the thin line that puffed cool oxygen into my mother's nostrils, and she opened clouded eyes.

"Hey there, pretty lady," I whispered. "I'm here."

She looked at me, smiled, closed her eyes, and whispered, "John." My father's name. "Dance with me." Her face puckered like a baby preparing to release a wail, then relaxed, and she was gone.

Joni drove us home, and as we headed north along Chicago's Lake Shore Drive, the world blurred: white slash of sails on the lake's slubbed surface, a soft puff of cloud, muted gleam of sun-burnished windshields. As we drove along the Gold Coast, past elegant old buildings that signify Chicago privilege past and present, Joni pointed out a single cloud shadow nestled over one high white building.

"Weird," she said. "Isn't that the building you lived in when you were little?"

"Not for long," I said. "Just while we were rich."

◆

I remembered little of the apartment where I spent my early years, but what I did remember was loud and bright. In the late 1920s, my parents were young and wealthy in a city that revered both virtues. Our home pulsed with heated politics, hot celebrities, and sizzling jazz that blended in one colorful blur. Parties were standard fare, bright and raucous, filling our days with gaiety. But of all the parties in that apartment, I only remembered two. And of those, only one was given by my parents.

It was 1929, an early Halloween celebration. I was six, but I still remember the music and laughter filtering up to the nursery, remember sneaking past my snoring nanny and perching halfway down the curved staircase that hugged the foyer. I could see the checkerboard floor below through the turned balustrades, black and white marble veined with wisps of silver and gold. People babbling in several languages made their way up and down the stairs, most ignoring me, but one woman wearing net fairy wings on the back of her flowing gown bent down to kiss my forehead, leaving behind a sugary scent. I rubbed my hand across the greasy lip print and wiped it on my pajamas, leaving a faint ruby trail down the pant leg.

An open arch framed the revelry in the ballroom across the foyer, and I peered, fascinated, at the people in bizarre costumes who drank my parents' liquor and smoked sweet-smelling cigarettes from tortoise-shell holders. Rapid bursts of music and laughter sprayed like machine-gun fire into the foyer. In the back, a heavyset woman was leaning against the piano, singing something about a good man being hard to find, while a young comedian from Waukegan tortured her with his screechy violin accompaniment to appreciative laughter.

White-coated servers glided to and from the kitchen, shoulders angled beneath trays of elegant dishes with hard-to-pronounce names. Lawrence, our dour-faced butler, was dressed as a jester in blue and yellow satin, complete with little bells that tinkled as he ushered the famous and fabulous beneath my nose. Years after, I might see a picture in a newspaper or magazine—Conrad Aiken, Bessie Smith, Sophonisba Breckinridge, George Gershwin, William Wrigley—and experience a flash of déjà vu of that same person seen from above, living flesh against black and white stone.

At one point, my mother emerged from the party. She carried a half-mask trimmed with peacock feathers, and her short blue dress shimmered like a waterfall as she walked. I was about to call to her when I recognized the little pout that signaled her annoyance over something. Realizing that she might not be amused at my being out of bed, I shrank back and kept quiet. An intense-looking young man with shiny, slicked-back hair lurched out from the party.

"Lily, Lily, Lily!" His voice was too loud, and as he leaned on her, she turned her head away from his face.

"Charles, you've had too much to drink. Let me call for your car."

"Dance with me, little Lily," the man pulled her to him and stumbled, pulling her around, as I stared.

"Charles, stop!" Mother pushed him away.

He tried again to kiss her then, and she slapped his face. I had never seen my mother raise a hand to anyone, and I jerked back as though I had been the one hit. Mother went to the front door and flung it open. Lawrence, looking amused, appeared with the man's hat.

"Go," she demanded. The man began to protest but stopped at her look. He grabbed his hat, bowed stiffly, and went out, leaving my mother standing there, breathing hard. She and I were both startled by my father's voice. Apparently, he had also been watching the little drama unnoticed.

"Another one, my dear?"

He, too, carried a mask covered with feathers, but like a parrot's. His long, creased face bore a quizzical smile that set his thin mustache at an amusing angle. Mother flitted to his side and grasped his arm, drawing him farther into the foyer, away from the party.

"Oh, John," she said, "I didn't—Do I make them think I—?" She looked up at him, a child seeking forgiveness. "John, I'm bad." Father's laugh boomed.

"I certainly can't blame them for falling in love." He kissed the tip of her nose. "Just make sure I'm the only one *you* fall for."

Mother snuggled up to him. "Never another."

Father held her at arm's length and gave her a mock-stern look. "Not even Fred?"

"Fred who?" Mother giggled and burrowed back against him.

"Fred," I knew, was the actor Fred MacMurray, from her hometown of Beaver Dam, Wisconsin. I had heard the story often, how she'd had such a crush on him that when he left for Hollywood, she packed up her broken heart and rode the train to Chicago, where she found a job selling men's furnishings at Marshall Field's. She met my father when he came in to buy some gloves, and they fell instantly, gloriously, in love.

Instantly, gloriously. Those were the words she used every time she told it, and it was easy to believe now as I watched my parents in the foyer below me. She snuggled closer.

"Dance with me, John." The band had stopped, but they started to dance to some private music, clinging to each other. All I knew as I watched was that my parents were happy, and a bubble of joy expanded in my chest, floating up to burst out in a giggle. Mother heard and turned to look up at me.

"Jack! You're supposed to be in bed!" She scolded as they both came up to join me on the staircase.

"Couldn't stay away from the party, eh, son? Well, that's my boy." My father picked me up and gave me a playful shake, then held me close, filling my nose with the familiar smell of bay rum. He smiled at my mother, who was stroking my hair. "So maybe there is another man in your life?"

"Yes, one more love," she murmured. "But that's because he's yours, too."

Another singer had begun, a woman with a low, smoky voice. We sat on the stairs listening, a single unit swaying together to the music.

◆

I had dozed off in the car, and when I awoke, we were pulling into our driveway in Winnetka. I reached over and patted Joni's hand. "Good thing you're driving, kiddo. I'd have plowed us into the lake."

"You were smiling in your sleep."

Caitlyn reached up from the back seat and slid her hand down my cheek. "Must have been a nice dream," she said.

◆

It had been a nice dream if a short one. That party marked the end of the life we had known. The market crashed a scant week later, and suddenly my father was broke. The parties ended, as did the calls from Mother's "friends." Bit by bit, our beautiful furniture and my mother's jewelry disappeared. Their sale bought us another year, but eventually, we had to give up the apartment for a less fashionable address farther north.

On our last day in the apartment, I was lying prone on the foyer floor, waiting for my parents to take me to a place with lower rents and darker realities. I lay with my cheek against the cool checkerboard floor, tracing the swirling patterns with my finger, trying to find the beginning or end of the golden veins that invariably faded away. Mother's best friend, Ludmilla Hancock, took over the apartment and servants, and she had hugged Mother, declaring her abject grief at taking advantage of our bad fortune before trotting off to plan her redecoration.

My father hauled the last of the trunks down the stairs and turned off the lights, leaving us in the faint glow of a half-moon rising over the lake, smiling at us through the tall windows as it always had, as though nothing had changed. We stood a moment looking around, and then Mother held out her arms to Father.

"Dance with me, John. Last dance?"

Wordlessly, Father enfolded her in his arms, and they moved gracefully in the moonlight while I watched.

"I'm sorry, Lily," he said finally.

"You'll find something."

He rested his head against hers as they spun around, and his voice was low as he said, "I'm not exactly qualified for anything."

He was right.

He dutifully followed every lead and called every contact, but there was nothing for him. In his old life, he'd never worried, but this new world presented new challenges and roadblocks. His education had prepared him to discuss Cicero's orations and identify time periods through music and art, but not to do anything concrete. Mother found a job first, as a waitress in a small restaurant near our "new" flat. My father protested, but as the weeks went by and his unemployment continued, his face set in tired resignation, the creases deepening. One night, as I padded past their door to the bathroom, I overheard them talking.

"You're demeaning yourself and me, working at that place."

"It's a paycheck. Plus tips." Mother said in an icy tone I didn't recognize.

"Oh, and do you shake your ass for a little extra?" Nasty, angry.

"John!" Shock.

"I'm sorry, Lil." Contrite. "It's just that—I should be taking care of you and Jack."

"I'm not keeping score. You'll find something soon." Father mumbled something I couldn't hear, and Mother's voice sounded weary. "Go to sleep."

There was no comfort offered, and as I stood there, the chill was from more than bare feet on a cold floor.

◆

Caitlyn and I went to clean out Mother's room at the nursing home, piling together the photographs of our children and grandchildren. Tucked in the back of the closet, Caitlyn found a large round hatbox that bore the distinctive logo of the long-defunct Mandel Brothers department store. Inside were carefully folded newspaper clippings, social columns from the 1920s in which my parents' names were prominently featured alongside those of many celebrities of the day.

"Oh, look at this." Caitlyn held up an old photograph, apparently taken on my parents' wedding day, but mounted behind a faded, hand-painted cardboard frame. The picture's sepia tone had darkened, and cracks ran across the top, but the couple gazing at each other was eternally young and happy. "How beautiful," Caitlyn said. "I've never seen this picture before." I stared at the photo.

"I have."

◆

Mother had managed to salvage a few things from the big apartment—a set of copper cookware, candlestick lamps her parents had given them as a wedding present, a pair of diamond engagement earrings from my father, and a sterling silver frame that held their wedding photograph, showcasing happier times.

There were a few other things as well, but as my father's unemployment continued, those, too, began to disappear, piece by piece, until only the pots and the frame were left, both glaringly out of place surrounded by the faded floral wallpaper and chipped porcelain sink. Many evenings, Mother would bring home a newspaper left at the restaurant, and while she attempted to pull together some cheap but filling meal, my father would read, just as he had always done. But where once he had read the listings of ever-climbing stock prices, he now scanned the less optimistic *Help Wanted* ads.

Mother was a terrible cook, and father's kidding about it often turned as sour as the milk. One day, when he joked that Mother must have roasted his old shoes instead of meat, she exploded.

"You don't like it, don't eat it. Better yet, cook for yourself!" She stood up quickly, jarring the table and knocking over a glass, which shattered on the floor.

She ran into their bedroom and slammed the door, shaking the walls and causing Mr. Reilly downstairs to bang on his ceiling and yell for quiet. My father sat without moving for a moment and then rose to get the broom and dustpan; he began sweeping up the shattered glass as I watched, despising him. That night when I went out to the bathroom, I heard him snoring on the sofa.

The next morning I entered the kitchen to find my father at the stove and my mother reading the paper at the table. I settled onto one of the mismatched chairs Mother had found in a thrift store to replace our more elegant, recently sold dining set.

"Ah, there's my little guinea pig," Father joked as he came at me with a spoon poised.

"Here, taste this oatmeal."

"I hate oatmeal," I turned my head away from the attack.

"You hate your mother's oatmeal," he said with a thin smile at her. "Try mine." My mother ignored us both, and I hesitated, unsure which side to take.

"Try it," Father demanded. "I made it. You eat it."

His voice forced me to comply, and I discovered it was indeed far better than the bland paste Mother always made.

"Want more?" he asked, and I looked at Mother, who shrugged.

"Of course he does. I'll have some, too," she said. As she went to the cupboard for bowls, she touched my father's arm, giving him a tender look that eased the tightness in my chest. "So, I'm a breadwinner, and you're a cook," she said. "The world has truly gone mad."

◆

I switched my formal education from private tutors to the local public school with the rest of the "great unwashed," a group we had unwillingly joined. My father stewed about the situation—he had attended the exclusive Parker School, and it grated on him that I could not. It became an obsession with him, even though I was perfectly happy at Alcott Elementary. Then one day, he came home ebullient. A few months earlier, he'd finally found work at a gas station in Evanston, and I was surprised to see him home so early. He swung me above his head, feigning surprise at my apparent growth, and laughed.

"You are going to go to Parker, my boy. No more ratty public school for my son!"

"What are you talking about?" Mother said.

"I dropped in on the director today! Explained that I was an alum. We chatted a while, and he agreed to take Jack on as a scholarship student."

"Oh, that's wonderful! Imagine! A scholarship!"

My father's smile tightened. "Well, it's not exactly a full scholarship. I'll also be working there as their janitor. It'll be less than I'm making now, but—"

"What?" Mother's newest frown line, a valley between her eyebrows, deepened. "How are we supposed to get along on that? His school is perfectly fine, and it's free. Work for half of nothing? What in hell were you thinking?"

I had never heard my mother swear before, and I retreated to my room, but I couldn't shut out the sound of their voices as their words got louder and uglier.

"I was thinking that my son needs an edge if he's going to be someone in this world."

"Someone like you? Fat lot of good your fancy education has done you! You'll work there for a little nothing, so you can't take a real job?"

"I'll find part-time work at night or weekends. We'll manage."

"Sure, as long as I keep slinging hash!"

Wrapping a pillow around my head, I ran down the list of U.S. presidents in my mind, but I could still hear their shouts punctuated by Mr. Reilly's pounding. Then a door slammed, and it grew quiet save for my own thumping heart.

The following week a large box was delivered, addressed to me. In it were a dozen Parker School uniforms of various sizes, leftovers donated by past Parker students. Even at ten, I could see that they were old and worn, but my father grabbed my mother, twirling her around the room, talking about my future glories. Afterward, she examined the uniforms and patted my cheek. "I can alter them," she said. "You'll look fine."

At Parker, I'd sometimes see my father in the hallways, leaning on a mop or a shovel, looking like a body whose soul had already departed. If he saw me—if I couldn't duck away quickly enough—he'd straighten up and wave, smiling, his brow lifted in anticipation. I never waved back. When I turned away, I tried not to imagine how his face must have fallen, how his eyes must have looked at his son's retreating back. But I continued to pretend I didn't know him. Once when I was walking with a group of guys, we overheard the headmaster berating my father for not washing a blackboard before the day's class.

"What a dope," the guy next to me said with a snicker. My ears got hot, but I tried to act nonchalant.

"Yeah," I agreed. "A real sap."

Then I ducked down a side hall and crushed myself into a doorway, pushing down tears as I fought humiliation and self-loathing, cursing both my father and myself for being who we had to be.

Those cruelties still haunt me.

Despite my ignominy, I liked the school and made some good friends. I was even invited to some of their homes, where each time I was reminded anew of what I had lost. I never brought my friends to my home, where my mother's stylish efforts couldn't disguise the fact that everything in the apartment was either cheap or used. Her efforts at decorating created the effect of a theatrical costume that appears elegant from a distance yet is revealed on closer inspection to have frayed edges and pulled seams.

I don't know even today if I was ashamed of our poverty or of my parents—especially my father. At first, he tried to retain some elegance, changing out of his coveralls into clean clothes each night. But after a while, he began to stay in his coveralls until bedtime. To save on toiletries, he would go days between shavings, sporting a perpetual spray of ashes across his chin. At night my parents would sit together on the shabby sofa as my mother rubbed cream into my father's chafed palms, but the hard work and cleaning chemicals were stronger than her efforts, and his once-manicured hands became rough and callused.

Mother finagled him the weekend shift as a cook at the restaurant, and I didn't see him much after that. Mornings, I slipped out for an early paper route before catching the streetcar, my carefully-folded uniform in a bag so I could change in the school locker room. I signed up for every after-school activity I could, in part to gain standing in the school, but also in part to prevent my father from waiting for me after school by the building's front door. I blamed him for our descent—not all of his friends lost everything—and hated him for being reckless with his finances. I watched my mother move from charming girl to charwoman, and I blamed him for that, too. I knew he was also hurting, but I didn't care. It had been his job to take care of us, and he had failed.

In my second year at Parker, Mother picked up the dinner shift at the restaurant, which meant longer hours but better tips. Father took over all the cooking at home, the results increasingly palatable as he worked to create economical yet tasty dishes. Each evening he had supper waiting and sat with me while I ate, pulling reluctant bits of my day out of me, himself not eating until later, when Mother dragged home. I'd sit in my room studying while they'd eat and talk. Once in a while, their laughter would seep through my closed door, and I'd stop reading to eavesdrop and remember.

We would listen to the radio and play a board game most evenings, or Mother would mend while we read. My father enjoyed reading aloud, especially Shakespeare, and he was impressive as Lear, Prospero, Henry, his resonant baritone filling the little room. Mother would put down her patching to watch him with bright eyes, and I could almost forget what he had been and what he had become.

Sometimes we'd go to the movies. As I got older and tried to refuse, Mother would beg me to go, and I'd grudgingly agree, although I always sat a row behind them. She especially loved Fred MacMurray's movies. The year 1935 had been good to the actor, and we watched him cavort with the likes of Katherine Hepburn, Claudette Colbert, and Carole Lombard. Afterward, as we walked home, Mother would exuberantly revisit the plot, the costumes, the hair, the scenery, and I wondered if she thought what life could have been like. From the way he looked at her, I guessed that my father was wondering the same thing.

There were times I could see the old John and Lily peeking through, but they were fleeting, teasing, and I almost resented them because they reminded me of what was gone.

Still, while our life wasn't exactly "Happy Days Are Here Again," it was tolerable.

Most of the time.

One night, Mother pushed away her plate after only two bites. "No more, please. I'm sorry, it's too salty."

He set his mouth. "Well, maybe you want the cooking duties back, huh? Or are you maybe eating at work to avoid my food?"

This struck me as funny, as though Mother was cheating on Father with food, and I laughed. It was the wrong thing to do. My father looked at me, his eyes wide and angry.

"Oh, you think that's funny? I work all day and then come home and try to make something nice for you, and you think it's funny?"

I backed into the living room. "Pop, listen—"

He followed, my mother fluttering in the background. "No, *you* listen! Both of you! I am doing my best, my best! And this—" he wildly indicated the shabby room—"*This* is the best I can do! You want to laugh?" He lunged for me, and my mother screamed. As I dodged his arm, he lost his balance and fell against the table that held the wedding photograph in the silver frame. The picture wobbled, and he grabbed it. I thought the world stopped as he stood looking at it. Then, with a savage yell, he threw it against the wall, the crash adding to the cacophony of my mother's shriek and Mr. Reilly's pounding.

Mother ran to pick up the frame, brushing her hand over the silver. She looked up at him, her eyes pleading. "Stop! If it's dented, I won't be able to sell it!"

My father's hard breathing and the pounding beneath us were the only sounds. Suddenly, he laughed, a sad, choking sound.

"So that's where we are, eh?" He grabbed his coat and stomped out of the apartment.

◆

The funeral director was cloying, pitching expensive coffins, and I felt overwhelmed by all the choices, but Caitlyn was firm.

"She wanted a plain coffin. Pine, with brass handles."

I looked at her, surprised.

Caitlyn squeezed my hand. "She asked me to take care of things when the time came and gave me specific orders. She knew you'd be a wreck."

I smiled at the thought of Mother planning to help me even after her death. "Okay," I said, "but make the lining soft of heavy satin. Blue."

I could take care of her, too.

◆

The government promised good times to come, and indeed, things did seem better for us. By the time I started the high school level at Parker, I had created a reputation for myself as a "right all-around guy." Even as a freshman, I was on the football and baseball teams and in the Drama Club and Debate. I had friends: guys impressed by my sports abilities, girls who thought I was "cute." I paid attention to what others in the school were wearing and saved my paper route money until I had enough to buy the "right" clothes, one piece at a time. My sophomore year, I picked up a second job, sorting bottles on Saturday mornings so I wouldn't have to ask for money to take a girl on a date. Everyone at school was talking about college already, and I worked doubly hard on my studies, knowing the only way I would go would be on a scholarship.

My father continued cooking, both for us and at the restaurant, and our meals kept getting better. Mother sometimes laughed at his intensity, calling him "Betty Crocker," after the popular radio cooking show.

They still danced, twirling to the radio. Although I pretended disdain, I would peek up from my homework, marveling at how smoothly they moved in our tiny living room. Sometimes they went to the Merry Garden Dance Hall on 25-cent nights, and when Mother got extra serving jobs at parties, they would splurge on an evening at the theater or the Aragon Ballroom. Dressed up in their best, if outdated, finery, they could blend into the crowded dance floor and forget for a little while the frays and patches of cloth and life. While they were gone, I found my own quiet pleasures in radio shows or, more likely, some depressing novel—there was a grim solace in reading books about people more miserable than myself.

One Sunday morning in June of 1937, my mother was preparing breakfast when the radio announcer gave the news that Fred MacMurray, now a major movie star, would be in the city for a visit.

"Eat your cereal," she said, her cheeks suddenly pink, and she started humming as she washed the dishes. She mentioned the news to my father as he lumbered to the table, still groggy with sleep.

"Big deal," he said. "Are we out of milk again?"

That night the phone rang, and Mother answered.

"Ludmilla! Oh, my God, it's been forever!"

"Lily, darling!" The other woman's voice was so shrill I could hear it crackling through the phone, even across the room. "I'm throwing a party, and I was wondering if you and John could be there."

"How wonderful!" Mother's voice was bright with excitement. "Oh, we haven't a thing to wear!" The other woman's voice grew quieter, and I couldn't understand her words, but Mother's entire body sagged as though under a sudden weight.

"Yes, Ludmilla, that will be fine," she said, her voice crisp. "Yes, of course, we'll be there. Thank you for thinking of us." She hung up the phone and left her hand resting on the receiver for a long time.

"Ma? What are you going to wear?" I asked.

"What?" She looked at me, unseeing, then suddenly came back into focus. "Oh! Well, Ludmilla said, of course, she will supply uniforms for us so we will look like the other servers." Her voice had an edge. "Isn't that thoughtful? How generous of her!"

I was concerned about how my father would take the comedown. In my mind, I imagined the conversation. Father offended and refusing, Mother insisting, rebuking him for his pride. I was sure that Mother would be the strong one, and I even wondered if Father would cry. When my father got home that evening, he was sneezing and coughing from a summer cold. Hiding from what would surely be a fight, I tried to concentrate on the words in *Oliver Twist,* letting Dickens' wretched orphans offer cold comfort.

Mother approached him with Ludmilla's offer, and I braced myself, but there was no explosion. In fact, when I looked up, Father had an amused look on his face.

"Sure, what the hell. It might be fun at that. And can you imagine the faces of our old friends as we pass them a tray?" He laughed but looked as though he was sucking a lemon. Then I heard him say the worst thing of all.

"Call her back and ask if Jack can work, too."

"Huh?" My head popped up.

"Come on, kid, you could earn enough money for a sweater like the one that Bates kid wears." My cheeks burned at the thought that my longing had been so obvious.

"That's a good idea." Mother patted my face, which must have looked horrified.

"Ma, I don't know how to serve people."

Her smile was grim. "It's an easy thing to learn."

I panicked. Some of my friends' parents might be at the party. What would they think? I looked at my parents, and considering how hard they both worked, I reached down to find some compassion. Instead, I found myself wishing I could just shove them away where no one I knew would ever see them.

Then shame washed over me to overcome the selfishness. I squared my shoulders. "Sure, Ma. I'll do it. And I only want half the money. You take the rest."

"That's my boy," my father grabbed me in a rough hug. "I'll make it up to you, Jack. To both of you. I promise."

My mother's voice was thick as she said, "For God's sake, John, don't give him your cold!"

◆

That was the second party I remember.

When I entered Ludmilla's apartment, I felt a sudden surreal recognition. The checkerboard floors were still there, but the large arch had been replaced by formidable-looking double doors, now flung open to the ballroom beyond where the once-bright red walls were now a muted beige. The light fixtures were different, too, ornate and ugly. The party music was sedate, the conversation quiet, and the thought that my parents' parties had been much livelier made me feel somehow better about the paradigm shift.

Father jumped into the role with all his acting skills, adopting a formal, aloof air and proffering silver trays of elegant bits as though to strangers. I had to admire his innate grace; even in his server's jacket, he cut a more elegant figure than any man there. No one spoke to him or even acknowledged his presence, and he played the game. Mother, however, plunged into the past, and I cringed as she tried to chat with old friends but was met with icy rebuffs. Social climbers who once hung on her every *bon mot* now turned away from her in mid-sentence, pretending they had never known her on the same side of the serving tray. After a while, Ludmilla grabbed Mother and pulled her into the foyer.

"For heaven's sake, Lily, stop trying to be familiar with my guests!"

"They used to be my guests, Luddie. I introduced you to most of them."

"I know, dear, but your place has changed."

The pair held a stare for a moment before Ludmilla looked away, and I caught a little smirk of triumph on my mother's face.

"Well, then, I'll be getting back to work now, *Mrs. Hancock.*" Mother lifted her chin and glided back into the other room with a tray of smoked salmon and cucumber curls.

As my parents and I served caviar-topped toast points, we heard someone mention that Fred MacMurray would be there. The anticipation of reflected celebrity mingled with the scent of Chanel and cigar smoke, and I saw a high color rise in my mother's face as she served.

Then the star appeared, handsome, dapper, and debonair, with his elegant wife, Lillian Lamont, on his arm. He was taller than most of the other men, dark hair perfectly in place, face with the familiar heavy jaw and cleft chin that filled the movie screens. The glittering couple entered the room, the man shaking all eager hands, his husky voice saying how good it was to be back in Chicago. With a little prodding and encouragement, he approached the band and took a proffered saxophone, joking about time and tide. The song he played was high and sweet and peppy, and afterward he acknowledged the applause with a humble bow.

On my way back to the kitchen, I saw my mother leaning against the ballroom door frame. My heart ached at how the unflattering cotton uniform hung on her thin frame. Her hair, wispy from the kitchen humidity, formed a soft golden halo around her starched white cap, and her face was peaked and drawn, furrows running across her forehead. The contrast between her and the exquisite women at the party was marked. Torn between humiliation and pity, between unreasonable hatred and pathetic longing, I considered pushing her back into the kitchen where she wouldn't embarrass herself—or me—further.

Her eyes stopped me: youthful, shining, the eyes of the wedding photograph. A small smile played about her lips, and she swayed slightly against the door. There was a sylph beneath the drooping cotton: passion, youth, beauty long subdued. I recognized in her the same longing as I had for an expensive sweater, for college, for success—all things yet to come for me, long gone for her.

I wasn't the only one watching her, and I saw my father off to the side, in his eyes a world of pain and humiliation. I wondered if it wasn't worse to have something and lose it than never to have it at all, and my embarrassment and pity changed into a newer, deeper pain I didn't understand and didn't like.

I couldn't stay sucked into their agony, and I turned to go. Just then, the guest of honor came through the archway, pulling a cigarette out of a gold case. He glanced at my mother, and she straightened, but he gave no hint of recognition as he leaned into his silver lighter.

"Fred?" Mother's voice was tiny, like a schoolgirl approaching the teacher's desk. The man looked up. "Fred, it's me. Lily Gra—Lily McCoy." She gave her maiden name, knowing he wouldn't know her married one.

The man smiled tolerantly, the studied smile of the oft-mobbed. "Well, hello there, Lily!"

He took her hand and shook it. "How very nice to meet you. You're all doing a bang-up job here tonight!" I felt an acrid taste rise from my stomach but stayed rooted to the spot, unable to look away, as one gapes at a car crash.

He was about to re-enter the ballroom but turned back with a kind smile.

"Say, would you like to dance with me?"

My mother nodded, mute. The big man stubbed out his cigarette and held out his arms. She flowed into them, a beatific smile on her face. They moved into the ballroom and did a couple of turns around the floor, the other dancers parting for them. I heard someone near the door say something about what a great guy he was, so nice even to the help, and I hoped she hadn't heard the remark. My father watched, too. The song ended, and the actor led his partner back to the foyer, where he lightly kissed her hand.

"Thank you, Lily. That was lovely." He turned to go back in, but my mother stopped him with a hand on his arm.

"Please—"

"Of course." He pulled a pen from his inside pocket, looking around the hallway for something to write on. Picking up a napkin from the hall console, he quickly jotted something on it and handed it to my mother. "Always glad to oblige a fan," he said, bowing slightly. "Excuse me." And he disappeared back into the crowd.

Mother stood there holding the autograph, watching him go. My father moved to her and placed a gentle hand on her shoulder. She stared at him for a heartbeat, then folded into his arms and began to cry, burying her face in his shoulder. They clung together, my father making little shushing noises until my mother's sobbing ceased. He tipped her face up to his and with his thumbs wiped her tears away, then leaned down and kissed her with a passion I had forgotten they shared. After a long look, they pulled apart and went back to work.

Later, jubilant with Ludmilla's money in our pockets, we left the building for the last time and turned north toward home. The waxing moon was high, its light all but lost in the amber cast of streetlights, and the cool air carried the fresh, fishy tang of Lake Michigan. My father talked nonstop, ideas bubbling in his head.

"Did you taste those hors d'oeuvres? I could make those. Hell, I could make anything she had there, probably better and cheaper, too."

Mother said, "Why don't you see if Artie will let you try some new recipes in the restaurant?"

"That's a good idea. He likes my cooking. Maybe I can talk him into some other ideas I've had. Maybe into doing some catering." He reached over and punched my arm. "Hell, we're all experienced servers now. Maybe I'll start a restaurant of my own! Make it a real family business. Once Jack graduates from Parker, I can quit there and start working for real, for myself. For us."

Another time I might have bristled at his suggestion that I was holding him back, might have grumped that I never wanted to go to that damn school anyway, but this time I kept quiet.

Maybe it was being at that party with my parents, seeing their classiness amidst all the phonies, their love above humiliation, or maybe it was just one of those fleeting moments of maturity. But as I looked at my father and mother, holding hands and laughing, Mother nodding as Father wove his cloth of dreams, I swallowed the bile and vowed to work even harder, maybe even graduate early. There was no anger, and no guilt left—just a heady new responsibility.

"Don't you want to take a streetcar, Lil?" Father asked. "You were on your feet all night."

"So were you. If you're fine, I'm fine. It's a beautiful night, and I, a mere serving girl, have danced with a movie star!" Her laugh was a little too high. "Wasn't that funny? He didn't recognize me!" She shrugged, and her voice turned sad. "I guess everyone changes."

Father pulled her to him and kissed her nose. "You haven't changed. Not in any way that counts."

Something almost imperceptible flickered across her face, then was gone, and she pulled away to skip ahead of us. "I want to dance!"

My father caught her arm. "I'm no movie star."

"No, you're real," she said, her voice serious. "And you're mine. So, dance with me."

They danced then, to music only they could hear, and I vaguely recalled the ghosts of another moonlit night. But these were no ghosts, and the light was more streetlamp than moon, the dancers more steel than gossamer.

Mother was buried next to my father at a small graveside service, attended only by our family. As the others left for their cars, Caitlyn and I stood, her hand laced with mine, gently swaying to silent music reinforced by time, familiarity, and example.

The Medal

The Medal was not presented every day, and the atmosphere in the waiting area set just off the presentation room was solemn as befitted the occasion. People in dark suits milled around, speaking in low voices into wires that curled around their ears. An occasional military uniform strode through, its wearer moving with conviction, all precise posture and measured steps.

The family—the father, the mother, and the son—sat together on a couch, the star participants, the reason for the event, yet removed as mere observers of the meticulous preparations around them. A woman with a solemn mien perched on the edge of a facing chair, giving instructions in a respectful, hushed tone, explaining the protocol, the steps the family would go through, what they should—and should not—do. The mother nodded and asked questions. The father did not speak.

On his left, leaning against the space that was once filled by a barely-remembered arm, the boy was playing a video game that emitted electronic blips, the soft "dings" surreal amidst the somber quiet. The man observed his son's absorption in the game, examined the intense concentration on a face not yet sharpened into manhood. The boy was, at thirteen, poised on a cusp, skin clear, upper lip smooth beneath a shadow more down than a mustache. He had been awed by the plane trip, the hotel, the limo, and now sat with the calm drawn from the faith of a child: faith in God, in country, in good.

The father's only faith was in this boy with a face like the one forever lost.

It was that other face—rather the absence of it—that had brought them here to this room, to the upcoming ceremony of respect. The father felt himself tilting, his asymmetrical body unbalanced on the worn, yielding cushions. The woman instructing them smiled and moved away; uncomfortable, he shifted his weight, listing to the right, and at the movement, his wife focused on him, her eyes anxiously searching his face as though seeking cracks in the valleys that mapped the landscape from eyes to mouth.

She ran her hand up to his shoulder and found a familiar spot on his neck, which she gently kneaded with her thumb. "Pain?"

He shook his head. "I'm okay." At least in my body, he thought.

"You look so tired," she said, then lowered her voice. "The dreams are back, aren't they?" She spoke low, so only he could hear. He had always appreciated her sense of decorum. "They were gone for a while."

"Sometimes they just come," he said. "I think of something—"

"Triggers. The doctor said there would be triggers."

"Ironic word for it."

"You should go back. He was helping."

"Some wounds aren't meant to close."

"Stop beating yourself up. It's not your fault."

"It doesn't matter."

"It was no one's fault. The decision was his own. You know how headstrong he is—was—" Her voice broke, and she bit her lip. Even after nearly a year, she still spoke of her older son in the present tense.

The father raised his arm, and his wife leaned under it against him, fitting into the curve of his body. A ceiling fan hummed lazily, rhythmically above them, the blips of the boy's game providing a metallic counterpoint. The fan offered little relief in the packed room, warm from the movement of many bodies. Voices buzzed through earpieces, and the toy plinked its tinny melody. The father struggled to remain awake, but his eyelids sank against his resolve. The fan blades hummed, the sound clicking, morphing...

We're running across the dense jungle floor, dodging "wait-a-minute" vines that clutch at us, snatching at our cammos. Chopper blades become insect hums become the rapid beat of gunfire punctuating our run. Tat-tat-tat, a baseball card stuck in bicycle spokes. Tat-tat-tat-tat-tat. Don't ride too far, son! Be home for supper! The short bursts stop as a mine goes off to my left, a white-hot blaze. I'm okay. It's only my arm. No pain. No sound. Where's Wally? Move out! Move out! Gotta find Wally! Men, shadows, cut through the humid haze, chimeras shooting fire in the pink mist, fading in and out, green on green, searching among the dead and wounded for buddies and bodies. Calls and moans: Medic! Jesus, O Jesus! Oh, God! Quiet, quiet down, be quiet. You seen Wally? Kid with the harmonica? The jungle air drips with sobs and gasps and blood, the hum of insects constant above it all—breeding season. We've been pulling them out of coffee mugs, cots, hair, and eyes. Now we're pulling them out of shreds of flesh, gaping wounds. The maggots will come later. The smell of char mixes with the jungle's heavy, damp, green smell. Bits of flesh dot the brush like scattered crumbs. Here, boys, toss these for the birds! That's right—Winter's tough on birds. You gotta take care of them. Have you seen Wally? I'm picking my way through the brush, my right hand pushing my gun through barbed vines, left arm hangs, mangled, useless, boots caked with red mud. Kid sitting against a rock, ragged edges where his legs used to be. Here, pal, here's my canteen. Have a drink. Kid thanks me politely like we're at a tea party. He drinks a swig, the light in his eyes goes out. It's a raccoon, boys. Must have been dead a week. Get a shovel, and we'll bury it. No, son, you don't have to look. I'll take care of it. Go back in the house. I'll take care of everything.

Where's Wally? Wally from Alabama, Wally with the harmonica. Bodies and parts of bodies litter the jungle floor, lying in rivers flowing red through the grass. It looks like Christmas, all that red and green. Hey, Pop, can we get a toboggan for Christmas? Sure, boys, I'll take care of it. The green shifts, and my feet sink into sand. There is no more jungle steam but a new kind of hot beneath a dry sun. The bodies are no longer green. Their uniforms are the color of the sand splashed with red. A glint—there, there! Sun on harmonica sticking out of a back pocket. I turn the body over to look at Wally's face, half gone, popped eye drooping onto his cheek. The face blurs, shifts, morphs. My son, it's my son.

The father jolted awake. The mother's hands flew to his shoulder, rubbing his back. His rapid breathing slowed. They were still on the couch, waiting to be led to the dais. The mother patted his shoulder and returned her hands to her lap, where she rubbed her nails, dry-scrubbing cuticles the color of a bruise, stained from peeling and cooking apples. She always laughed that she should wear gloves but never did. He had seen her scrubbing her nails with a brush in the hotel, but the shadows remained. They'd have to wear away in time. He put his big hand over hers, covering the discolorations.

A commotion indicated the Leader's arrival, who appeared amidst the flash of cameras.

Get down! Get down! Where's Wally?

The father's arm jerked at the bursts of light, but he caught the reflex. A river of heat ran up his back and circled his neck; he breathed deeply and turned from the flashes.

The Leader moved toward the family, and the three rose as one. The mother's hands flitted to smooth her skirt and hair, and the Leader caught one and leaned in to kiss her cheek. He extended his right hand to the father, who felt an ember spark in his chest and tamped down the desire to jerk his hand away. This man had been his son's commander-in-chief. A thin thread of something half-forgotten tickled his brain, and his back straightened, obeying a near-forgotten reflex.

"I'm truly honored to meet you," the Leader said. "Your son was a real hero, a credit to our proud nation."

"Thank you." Acceptable.

The Leader's eyes were narrow and looked tired beneath the slightly hooded brow. The father experienced a flash of disembodied eyes seen through a slit of a tank turret, felt the same quick rush of fear and distrust, but tamped it down.

"Your family has a proud history of serving your country," the Leader smiled. He turned to the boy who stood hushed at his father's side. "And does this young man plan to enter the military too? To be a hero like his father and big brother?"

The boy's face carried something unreadable—Hope? Fear?—and the father felt the ember flare.

"No!" His voice too sharp, too loud as he angled his body in front of the boy as if to protect him. The Leader flinched, and one of the silent men at the Leader's side jerked his hand to his jacket, revealing a glint of steel. The fire burned in the father's chest, but he swallowed it down. "No." He spoke softer. "No, he's just thirteen." The Leader nodded. The two men assessed each other across the gaping silence, men who both knew great loss, thought the father.

"Well, they're waiting for us." The Leader signaled a pair of Marines who had been standing at attention near the door. *Boys,* the father thought, looking at their serious faces. *No, men.* The pair moved with sharp steps, ushering the group into the presentation room. The Leader strode to the podium, his face an appropriately solemn mask. Then he turned to the family as they entered and sat in a neat row beneath the gold and blue seal that dominated the platform. Along one side of the platform stood three men and one woman in dress uniforms, all at attention. Cameras flashed like lightning bugs.

The father listened once more to the story that had been in all the papers, on television, radio, the Internet. He'd heard it all before, lived it. A mine. Quick thinking. Saved lives. Selfless. A hero. He knew he'd had his time to grieve, that this was merely a formality, a necessary recognition, a rite. Still, the pain, always just beneath the surface, felt fresh. This was strictly ceremony, and it meant nothing. He had agreed to come for his wife, his son.

His sons.

He was surprised that it was over so quickly. The Leader handed the mother the flat leather case and reached out to shake the father's hand once more, then leaned in to give the mother a peck on the cheek, his face strategically turned for the proper photographic angle. The father saw his wife turn her head slightly away from the embrace, slipping her hand out of the Leader's, and her eyes met her husband's, his pain mirrored. The cameras continued to snap, lights and clicks in short bursts like machine gunfire. His mind slipped, shifting slightly, as the room tilted for just a moment.

Tat-tat-tat-tat-tat. I'll be home in time for supper, Pop!

It was over. The gathered audience moved around, talking or texting, checking their cameras, jotting notes. The Leader smiled and chatted with the uniformed men and women. The father waited respectfully for the Commander-in-Chief to turn to him. Some cameras were still clicking. The Leader waved to them slightly, then came up to him.

"It was an honor to meet you all," the Leader said.

"Thank you, Sir." That was enough.

"Your son was a true hero. A credit to you, to our great nation."

"Thank you." Again. What else was there to say? He swallowed the fire that threatened to consume his chest, to burst out and engulf the room.

A guard whispered something to the Leader, who turned to go. The flame demanded a quench, and the father reached up to touch the man's arm, pulling him back slightly.

"You have no children in the military," the father said, a statement rather than a question. He had not meant to say it so loud. The buzz around them lowered suddenly. The Leader froze, then turned. His face remained unchanged but washed pale. The turret eyes shifted, almost imperceptibly.

The Leader looked at him, his eyes unyielding, and for a millisecond, the father was startled by their heavy sadness. "They're all my children." He nodded to a young Marine, who stepped up alongside them.

"Sir?" the young man extended his arm to indicate the way to move. The father turned to go. The mother was waiting near the door with their son, and the leather box clutched to her chest.

A silent guard waited to escort the family through the halls to where a car waited to take them back to their hotel.

"A medal," the mother murmured, her voice low, thick. "A reminder. That's what it'll be, always. As if we needed one."

A group of young men in uniforms were gathered in the hallway. Their faces were strong and handsome. Like Wally. Like his son, his sons. These boys were someone's sons, too. Would one of them someday have a family in the waiting room? Looking at them, so willing and selfless, the father felt the fire inside him change, became not consuming but warming.

As his little group approached, the young soldiers suddenly snapped to and saluted, and he realized The Leader was walking behind him. He turned to see the Leader salute heard him quietly say, "God bless you all."

The Leader turned to the father then and saluted him. The father looked at the Leader standing there, eyes straight, waiting. In that moment passed decades, years, days, seconds, all the same. *When I grow up, I'm gonna be a hero like you, Dad.* The father glanced to the side and saw his young son was watching with familiar eyes—his brother's eyes. What had he taught that boy? Children learn what they see their parents live.

The father's back straightened, and his hand snapped up to return the salute.

South Shore, Chicago

The old neighborhood was nearly unrecognizable. I hadn't been back in South Shore since my family left, suburban-bound in station-wagon trains, moving away from the tight little ghetto that had welcomed them, immigrant by immigrant, from the pogroms and the prejudice of the Old Country. Now, pulled by a need to see where I began, I've veered off the expressway to travel back, in time and place.

Yet time has not been kind to my childhood home. The sidewalk that bore the tread of family feet is now buckled, yielding to the roots of gnarled trees that line the broken way, their shadows specked with unexpected light. I could close my eyes and follow the path I walked every Saturday morning, every holiday, on my way to synagogue. As I walk, I can count the slabs, stopping at the one that still bears two small handprints: my cousin's and mine, forever embossed in the cement beside our names, scrawled in a childish hand. I smile, remembering how we kneeled by the soft, new cement, giggling in our pleated skirts and knee socks, scuffing our "shul shoes" on the rough ground as we froze that moment, dedicating our youthful selves to time and cement.

Coming down the alley, my mother saw us in our evil deed. "On yontiff you do that?" she sighed, and then, laughing as she wiped our hands of shame, she kissed our foreheads, lovingly as God. How warm, that kiss, in memory, though long cold the lips!

How alive still the remembrance of light and white and fringe and prayer, remaining warm within me.

South Shore in the 1950s was a family neighborhood—my family. Summer evenings were accompanied by the soundtrack of traffic on 79th St., two blocks south, the hum punctuated by the periodic roar of the El that rattled the tracks. Across the street, the armory loomed above all, a symbol of protection in an uncertain world. Tall lamps cast a rosy glow as people strolled to escape the heat of steamy homes and flats in summer or ran bundled against the buffeting winds in winter. I would watch the people from my window and enjoyed the security of knowing that many of them were my family. But of course, even those not related were well-known and family.

But the safe comfort has been gradually worn away by time and change, as even the hardest stone is reduced, bit by bit, imperceptibly, by wind and water. The family fragmented and parted, running away from the unfamiliar to the suburbs, south, west, no longer tightly bonded or within walking distance.

What had once been home, the air warm and clear as the autumn sun, had once been clean, now rolled like a mangy dog in the dust of neglect. Worn houses, once straight and neat, now crouch like aging, broken beasts, bent with age's curse of sagging spines and shedding coats of paint. Everywhere seeps the scent of anger, a smell as hot as blood, an odor that slinks the streets like an exfoliant surreptitiously dusted, commingling with the filth of russet dust, of unswept leaves pulverized by time and tread.

So is the neighborhood I loved laid low since my cousins and I could safely walk about at night, chasing the chimes of the ice cream truck or kicking a ball in the street. I know it's foolish for me to be here, know that I should reclaim the safety of my car, but need and memory drive me on to my destination, just ahead: The synagogue, still square and stone, still there, still stoic through time's devastation.

It's changed little, yet changed completely. Once decorated with a wooden Star of David, its door now boasts a plain, shining cross. The windows, once a pastel rainbow of whorled panes, are now pained by change, some replaced with splintered wooden boards that press like bandages across a wounded cheek.

I remember sitting on my family's balcony, next to my mother, looking below at the white-shrouded men praying around the little square *bima*. I wonder if the chandeliers remain, great ivory glass lights that hung down beneath a circle of bright bulbs, inverted like a Hasid's fur-trimmed hat. As I sat lulled by the drone of words familiar yet unknown, staring at those great, hanging lights, I'd imagine myself launching from the brass safety rail, swinging by the light's metal chains, across the top of the room, landing safely on the curved ledge of the high windows on the opposite wall, round and blue bays with white-glass stars, matching the blue stars on the chandeliers.

As I grew older, I left my dreams of swinging on the lights to contentment in simply being in such a hallowed place, surrounded by love and family. I could picture God watching us from the high, curved white ceiling. When we read (the

English translation) in the prayer books of how He would decide who would live and who would die, who from stoning and who from drowning, I could feel His presence, and I wanted so desperately for Him to love me and inscribe me in His Book of Life. Each time I visited the little shul, I vowed to be a better person, a better Jew, to give tzedakah and grow in His glory. Each time I left, I left renewed, my outlook refreshed, my soul replenished.

Like wind and rain on a rock, time wears away piety. I left that cherished enclave for a wider world. My family left, the neighborhood "changed." My mother died, and with her died my devotion. I raised my sons to believe in tradition, but more to believe in themselves and their responsibility to the world—not just to religion. I lost a little of myself, and now I return to find that piece, that peace.

As I approach, two teens, lounging on the steps, turn to look at me, their dark eyes wide with questions.

"You lost?" one asks. Her friend gives her a nudge, and they both laugh.

"No, I'm okay, thanks," I smile. They're just kids. "Just visiting."

They shrug and stand to go in, leaving behind the shadow of a covert glance. I remember those glances given in this neighborhood long ago—only now I am the recipient.

Soft music begins inside—a choir practice, I guess. It swells, building like a wave in rhythmic prayers, blending with autumn wind, a song to grace a graceless world. The music morphs in my mind, becoming something old, remembered remnants, shards of sounds that recall bending nasal tones and plaintive chants. It's there within our mortar, buried deep, the dance of language that lingers, drawing deep of autumn nights and prayers that vivified, even if only half-understood. My own roots, tangled, complex, grew here, where concrete and ethereal combined.

For many years I walked the bidden path, bound with the strong rope of generations; bound by sound and soul, by threads of heart and hand. Now, though much is gone—the house, my mother, youth—this canon, even sleeping, stays alive.

The music soars in the autumn air. It is joyful, hopeful, loving, even as our chants were filled with joy, with hope, with love. Time may change the face of salvation, yet salvation remains, even as the words, tones, and rhythms alter. The songs today still carry the same dreams still offer solace, hope, familial warmth. The melodies of this place, today and past, combine and shift, first one and then the other, the same and not the same, the melody sweet and strong in bend and beat. The purpose is new and yet not new, for faith is faith and true in any form. Within those walls, belief is safe; the name means nothing, the symbols merely that. The heart is all.

A police car pulls up to the curb and stops. The window rolls down, and the officer asks me if I'm lost, offers me a ride away to somewhere safe. I thank him and say I am visiting relatives. He nods skeptically and rolls his window back up, and drives slowly away.

The singing draws my ear as the rainbow windows and blue-and-white stars once drew my eyes. Down the path, ancient trees with tangled roots stretch beneath the sidewalk, beyond fear. This place has changed and yet remains the same, timeless, passing from each to each.

It's time to leave behind the cement and the brick, knowing that the road that brought me here will take me home at the last.

Acknowledgments

First of all, I offer unbounded thanks to my publisher, Jerry Brennan, and my editor, Ta'teonna Payne, for their guidance and patience with me, and Tortoise Books for the willingness to take a chance on an old broad with a dream.

I thank the editors at the various magazines and Web sites who first published some of the stories printed here, including Cicada for publishing "The Difference" and "The Gift;" EscapeIntoLife.com for "The Mikvah;" The First Line for "South Shore, Chicago;" and JerryJazzMusician.com, for "Plainsong."

My great appreciation goes to my professors, mentors and colleagues at Northwestern University, including Patrick Somerville, John Keene, Miles Harvey, Sandi Wisenberg, Tara Ison, Reginald Gibbons, and Jennifer Companik for their guidance and encouragement.

I remember with love my parents, Matt and Judy Becker, who knew me better than I knew myself, and were wise enough to direct me along the right path, and my late husband, Richard, for pushing me into grad school, telling me, "It's your turn." And my thanks go along with my heart to Will, Sarah, Joe, Courtney, Matthew, Henry and Eva for being my strength and my foundation of love and support.

Finally, I extend my gratitude to the memory of Judy Dalton, the teacher who told a goofy teenager that she was a writer—and changed her life.

Publication Information

"The Difference" was first published in *Cicada* in 2006.

"The Gift" was first published in *Cicada* in 2011.

"The Mikvah" was first published on EscapeIntoLife.com in 2012.

"South Shore, Chicago" was first published in *The First Line* in 2015.

"Plainsong " was first published on JerryJazzMusician.com in 2018.

About the Author

Prior to earning her MFA from Northwestern University, Joyce Becker Lee worked as a newspaper reporter, editor, theater columnist, textbook developer, and high school and college instructor of English, Writing, and Theater. Her stories, features, and poetry have been published extensively in print and online, and she also writes novels, plays and screenplays. A dedicated theater enthusiast, she has spent a lifetime in educational, community, and professional theater as a director and performer, and is writer/composer of seven children's musicals. She enjoys volunteer work for civic and animal-related causes and is a busy hands-on grandmother.

About Tortoise Books

Slow and steady wins in the end, even in publishing. Tortoise Books is dedicated to finding and promoting quality authors who haven't yet found a niche in the marketplace—writers producing memorable and engaging works that will stand the test of time.

Learn more at www.tortoisebooks.com or follow us on Twitter: @TortoiseBooks.

CPSIA information can be obtained
at www.ICGtesting.com
Printed in the USA
JSHW031933090323
38720JS00001B/1